EARTH ENDURES 2

BLEAKER

JACQUELINE DRUGA

PRESS

VULPINE
PRESS

Published by Vulpine Press in the United Kingdom in 2021

ISBN: 978-1-83919-370-5

www.vulpine-press.com

Also by Jacqueline Druga:

What we Become

Like many, Mackenzie Garret complains about the weather. It is the hottest summer anyone can remember. The high temperatures are out of control with no end in sight. Until it all changes.

Overnight, blue skies become gray, and the hot, humid weather turns to rain, then snow, then ice as the temperature plummets.

The entire northern half of the country is thrown into chaos as blow by blow, storm after storm, nature rips into the world, tearing it apart. Towns and cities are evacuated, and Mac and her family are forced to leave their world behind and face a treacherous journey south to safety.

Will they make it, or will they be left behind in this new, frozen world?

Omnicide

A town practically cut off from the rest of the country, Griffin is always the last to know about everything. Fax is the most reliable method of communication and the local newspaper is the main source of outside information.

When a freak car accident occurs on the outside of town, no one thinks much of it. That is until deer are found sick and covered in an unusual growth, and they lose contact with the next town.

Cut off and isolated from the rest of the world, Griffin is unaware of the threat growing outside the safety of their little town. One that could endanger their entire existence.

PART ONE: Omni-4

ONE

The Ship

The clean, white surface was tattered and worn, yet even the natural devastation couldn't topple the Washington Monument. The stone had broken down, the triangle top looked as if it had crumbled, but it was recognizable to the crew of the Omni-4 as they made their first flyover of Washington, D.C.

Aldar Finch was stone-faced, trying not to show emotion when he saw his nation's capital far from the glory it was in its heyday. It crushed him, gnawed at his insides and the only thing that made it the tiniest bit tolerable was that mankind didn't do it to itself.

Nature did. But nature didn't rebel on its own. It was a forced evolution of Earth's surface. A planet had made its way into Earth's gravity field, bringing devastation and destruction during its entire journey across the solar system. It became fiercer the closer it came.

Earthquakes, tidal waves, volcanic eruptions.

Seaboard cities crumbled to dust and entire states sank.

No one really knew that the rogue planet was the cause. At least when Finch and his crew left Earth. To the experts

1

and everyone else, it was just an expedited and violent form of Earth changing.

That rogue planet, known to some as Planet X, was considered nothing but a myth. A conspiracy theorist's wet dream and the tinfoil hat club's online video goldmine. It was a laughable notion. Really. They knew there was nothing out there that they couldn't see. Especially something as big as a planet.

How wrong they were.

They were wrong about a lot of things.

The entire mission, the development of the Omni-4 spacecraft, was to find a suitable home for Earth's inhabitants. A second Earth.

Project Noah.

And they thought they had found it when a satellite, believed to have been destroyed in 1993, suddenly appeared again with photographs of a lush and fertile planet.

The satellite had not been lost or destroyed; it had travelled through a wormhole that scientists speculated opened every twenty-five years. That speculation was never grounded until the weather satellite NOAA-13 returned.

Wormhole Androski was the portal to this mystery planet, the answer to man's extinction and a beacon of hope.

And so it began.

The Omni would travel through while the opportunity existed, confirm the presence of the planet and its habitability, and return to Earth.

Construction also began on larger crafts for when the portal opened again in twenty-five years. Those ships would take colonists to prepare the planet for the ARCs that would carry a small, selected percentage of Earth's population.

The doorway was open, the project was launched, Omni-4 flew through.

Find the planet, explore, and return home.

That was the mission.

Only, the crew of Omni-4 discovered they were already home.

The wormhole wasn't a portal to another galaxy, it was a portal to another time.

The crew landed one hundred and sixty-seven years after they left.

Earth had changed drastically, and Planet X was another moon in the sky.

The Androski had no guarantee; if they went back through it was a crap shoot, a lottery, on when they would arrive.

So they stayed.

They would explore their new home, their old word, and see what had become of it.

Their first stop: Washington, D.C.

TWO

The Crew

Aldar Finch, Commander

"Where should we put her down?" Curt Henning reached up to the controls from the co-pilot seat.

"Does it matter?" Finch asked.

"Actually..." Nate Gale leaned forward. "As the geological expert I will say it does matter." He played with his tablet computer, pulling up images. "I'd say the entire area east of the city is probably unstable." He turned to look at Westerman. "What do you think?"

Westerman wasn't a scientist. Far from it. He was eighteen years old but he had one advantage all the education in the world couldn't give Omni-4: Westerman had been born on the changed planet. His parents were part of the Genesis, the colonists that left Earth after Omni-4, but arrived on the new Earth decades before them.

"You mean, do I think it will shake and break?" Westerman asked.

"For lack of better words," Nate said, "yes."

"Probably not. It's only unstable the closer you get to the ocean. Then again, it's earthquake season."

"Earthquake season?" Nate questioned. "I've heard of tornado season, hurricane season, never earthquake season."

"Sure, don't know why. But there is. Earthquake, tidal wave, volcano season..."

Curt laughed. "What about winter, spring, summer, and fall?"

"Them too, but probably not like you remember. Not at least like my dad said."

Finch thought at that moment how there was so much to learn from the young man. Even basic stuff like weather patterns were more than likely second nature to him.

There were a few more moments of debate on where to land the craft and Finch settled on an area that wasn't without bumps, but it would work. A long, wide strip of dead land that he knew was once the Potomac River.

Nate Gale, Geologist

The moment Nate stepped off the Omni and his foot rested upon the hard soil, he flashed back to his school days and how he learned every professor and scientist was wrong about Washington, D.C.

D.C. was built on a swamp, they said.

Nate believed that.

They all said one day it would turn back into a swamp. That it would eventually, possibly, sink.

He even had a professor make political humor out of the fact that the government was built over a swamp.

Nate didn't get into political humor.

Actually, Nate didn't get into politics, it just wasn't his thing.

5

Washington, D.C., long since abandoned, long since slammed by disaster after disaster was far from a swamp.

He stomped his foot a couple times on the soil.

"Are we good?" Finch asked. "It's not going to sink is it?"

Nate shook his head. "No, we're fine."

He pulled out his sunglasses. Not that it was particularly sunny, but they cut the glare on his computer tablet.

He used an old map of Washington and created an overlay of the area the ship photographed before landing.

He lined it up to get an idea of where he was.

Although it wasn't hard to distinguish the capital and any of the other monuments, he wanted to be able to zoom in if they came across something else, to know exactly where they were. Not every place was a famous landmark.

After peering down at his tablet, he made a note. The area wasn't as overgrown as it should have been.

That told Nate more than Westerman had known—that the area had been hit a lot. Perhaps by storms.

They weren't near the ocean, but you wouldn't know that by the huge ship that was infused with the dirt on the outskirts of the city.

The land had grown around it, the ship was part of the earth now.

"Where to?" Nate heard Curt ask.

"Huh?" Nate peered up. "Are you asking me?"

"I'm asking anyone," Curt said. "Westie." He nudged Westerman. "Any thoughts on which way to go?"

"Nope. Never been here," Westerman said. "This is part of the Verboten zone. No one comes here. So I'm game."

"How about this," Finch suggested. "We know where we left the ship. Let's just not worry about a plan. We don't have a time frame. We just walk. See what we find out."

"Like tourists," Curt joked.

6

"Yeah," Finch grumbled. "Like tourists."

Sandra Anderson, Physician/Surgeon

She had been on the battlefield repairing injuries, but never had something caused Sandra to cry as she did when she saw Washington, D.C.

It broke her heart. It was a reiteration that everything she knew and loved had come to an end.

Sandra was selected for the mission based on her medical experience, her years as a soldier and the fact that she had no one in her life, as far as family went.

Yet, when they learned they had gone ahead to the future through the wormhole, she voted to try it again. To go back through the Androski. Take a shot to see if they could go back home to their time. Wormholes, though, weren't reliable.

For all she knew she could end up further in the future or further in the past

Her fellow crew member Curt brought up the point. Even if the Androski dropped them right back in the time frame in which they left, was it fair to go back without all the knowledge they could?

Was it fair to go back and say, 'This is what happens' instead of 'Here are the facts, take a look, what can we do'?

When she cast her vote, she had that plan in the back of her mind. She and Curt had discussed it.

In case going back through the Androski was something they eventually ended up doing, Sandra would gather all the information she could before they left. She asked Rey if she could take over the reins of video operator, at least while they were in D.C. Sandra would get footage to serve as proof or historical documentation.

They, like Finch said, were tourists. Albeit in the post-apocalypse, and just like any good tourist, Sandra was hoping to get lots and lots of images.

Curt Henning, Co-pilot

Was it a sign? The tip of Curt's boot hit what looked like a frosted sea glass version of a whiskey bottle. He lifted it, holding it up to the sun, watching it sparkle due to the colors from the light. It had been crystallized from the ocean salt, but it was a whiskey bottle nonetheless. Almost as if fate was saying to him, 'Yep, the world ended, but yours pretty much ended via the bottle long before Planet X caused its damage.'

Curt wanted to be on the mission, he really did. He wasn't Finch's first choice, and rightfully so. He had lost Finch's trust long before the mission was assigned.

Curt was an alcoholic. In his mind, he would always be one. Even though he learned to control his drinking, his life of not drinking never lasted long. Mainly because he was merely sober and not living in sobriety.

For the longest time, drinking controlled him. There were fewer days when he wasn't drunk than when he was. He doused his coffee with bourbon. The day his world came crashing down and reality set in, wasn't from hitting rock bottom, it was from fear of Finch.

Curt had slept in. It was the morning of a test flight in which he was flying with Finch. He had stayed on base, woken still intoxicated from the night before, and in a rush made his way down to the testing area.

Once he took his seat in the test craft, Finch knew.

"Are you drunk?" Finch asked.

Apparently, he reeked of alcohol. And Curt had to own up that he wasn't sober.

Finch lost it. He could have had Curt's job, but instead he told headquarters that Curt was ill. He followed up telling Curt that if he ever found him drinking behind the controls of any moving vehicle, he would beat him.

That was what Finch said.

Beat him.

For two years Curt didn't drink a drop. Nothing.

Stone-cold sober.

Then the world started falling apart and Curt didn't care anymore. He drank again, but he controlled it. During the fall-apart years, Curt regularly graced magazine covers. He was praised as a hero because he seemed to always be in the right place at the right time. He'd earned the name The Clutch for grasping someone and saving them seconds from death.

None of that mattered to Finch. To Finch Curt was a drunk, whether he was a sober hero or not.

In essence Finch was right.

Curt wasn't a hero. In his mind he was a coward because he didn't want to face a dying world without a bottle in hand.

Yet, there he stood, looking at the remains of a once glorious city with an empty bottle in hand, and if it had something in it, Curt probably would have drunk it.

It was a reminder that no matter how many years they skipped, Curt wasn't getting away from any of it.

Ben Vonn, Engineer

"Seriously?" Ben shifted his eyes to the bottle that Curt held in his hand. "All this and you lift a bottle."

"I was just…I mean look at it," Curt said. "It's absolutely beautiful."

"Yeah, I guess so," Ben replied.

While not many knew of Curt's problem, Ben did. And it angered him. Curt took for granted everything. He would have given anything to have been Curt for one moment.

To be able to clutch someone from death.

Ben would have chosen the moment that his house was swallowed by a sink hole. When Ben held on to the banister of his home and watched his sons fall over him into the pit below.

Ben reached for them, but he wasn't fast enough.

He wasn't Curt.

He wished he were.

Maybe it was for the better.

Which son would he have grabbed?

He lost them both that day.

Now the decay of the city was nothing to Ben. It held almost an odd beauty. He watched Curt drop the bottle and move ahead.

They were all moving, just walking. Nowhere in particular. No direction. They had just emerged from the former bed of the Potomac river which was probably where Curt found that bottle.

When they were flying overhead, Ben recalled thinking D.C. looked like some sort of lost city in a forest, with the Washington Monument being the beacon flagpole. But once they moved closer, the foliage wasn't as thick as he thought it would be.

Emerging from the riverbed, so much came into view. The buildings were mostly still intact. Some showed signs of being weather worn, some of earthquake damage. But every one of them was still recognizable.

At least to Ben.

A whole new generation would never know the city.

He thought of his own sons and their trip to the nation's capital.

His sons, or rather the loss of them, was the reason Ben had joined the mission. Though he never said it, Ben had plans of his own. Once they arrived on the new planet, he was going to stay. Even if he had to sneak off and disappear, that was his plan. He'd had no intention of returning to their Earth. No intention of going back to the place that caused him so much pain. Yet, there he was. There was no escape from any of it.

None at all.

Reyanne Harper, Teacher

She stood in awe of him, just the same as she did when she saw the Lincoln Memorial for the first time in fourth grade.

He was larger than life to her, and despite the century that had passed, the wrath of nature that befell Washington, D.C., the statue of Lincoln sitting in that chair was still precious to her.

As an educator, she adored him. She loved history and had studied Lincoln.

It meant a lot to be standing there.

With everything that had happened, some things remained.

The face of the monument hadn't worn, and she stared at him. Rey could hear his voice, or at least the voice she had given him in her mind. A deep, resonating voice telling his people, "You cannot escape the responsibility of tomorrow by evading it today."

11

That was always one of her favorite Lincoln quotes. She knew in her time they'd done all they could to fix 'tomorrow,' but she wondered if the generations before her, if they'd known, would they have done something? If so, would she be standing there in the pits of a dystopian world?

Was there anything that could be done? After all, a rogue planet caused it to all unfold.

The questions slipped from her mouth, not intentionally, but as if she were secretly talking to President Lincoln. "Would anybody be able to stop it? Would it be worth try-ing?"

Rey was staring so intently she never noticed Finch ap-proach. He did a sideways lean into her and whispered, "I don't think he'll answer you."

Startled, Rey jumped a little with an "Oh."

"I'm sorry."

"No, that's okay," she said. "I was just…thinking out loud, literally."

"About?" Finch asked.

"Stopping all this.

"Stopping…all this?" Finch repeated.

"Could they?"

"Who knows." Finch shrugged. "I mean when we left, we had no idea it was a planet causing it. Maybe if they'd known a hundred years earlier…maybe science could have come up with a way."

"Or move people."

"Move people where?"

"You heard Quinn," Rey said. "There were areas never touched by the wave or disasters."

"Maybe we need to go to those places."

"I would think the Genesis settlers did already."

"He didn't mention it," Finch said. "Might be worth it. Could be an entirely different ball game."

"What else is there to do other than sightsee a broken world?"

"It's not broken," said Finch. "Just different. What, um...were you asking Lincoln?"

"Well, I was just thinking about a quote of his. It deals with fixing what you can for tomorrow."

"You can't escape the responsibility of tomorrow by evading today."

"Yes. That's it," Rey said brightly.

"I know it well. Kind of fits. If you know something is going to happen tomorrow, don't ignore it today."

"And we didn't," Rey said. "We were trying to find a future. My question about stopping it was to him. What if he knew?"

"He wouldn't have believed it. We would probably be burned at the stake as witches or something."

Rey nodded. "I know you made the decision that majority rules, but I still think we should have tried to go back. Just my thoughts."

"Me too."

Quickly she looked at him. "Really?"

"Oh, yeah, I voted to go. You and I, and I am gonna guess Nate or Curt. But I made the call and we're here. Who knows? Maybe everyone will change their mind before the Androski closes back up and we can—"

"Finch!" Curt called from distance.

Finch turned around to see Curt making his way toward them.

"Hey," Curt said, slightly out of breath as he approached. "Hey, we..." He looked up to the Lincoln Statue. "That's cool."

"What is it?" Finch asked.

"Nate wanted you," Curt said. "You know how he said it has been a while since anyone has been in D.C.?"

"Yeah." Finch nodded.

"Well, that's wrong. Come and take a look," Curt said, then turned and started leading them down the memorial stairs. "Not only has someone been here recently, it looks like they were camping out and are probably still in the area."

"Are they native to the area?" Finch asked.

"Or maybe it was the other half of Quinn's people," Rey suggested. "He said they separated."

"He also said they don't come near here. It's the forbidden zone or whatever they call it," Curt replied. "They avoid it because it was, at one time, dangerous."

"How can we be sure?" Finch asked as they approached where Nate and the others stood. He then spoke directly to Nate. "We were speculating that the Genesis group is here. The ones that separated from Quinn."

Rey added, "They could be dangerous."

Nate shook his head. "No, it's not them. They were a larger group. This is one or two people, and it's interesting enough that I think we need to find them. But they may be back for this." He handed them what looked like a small handheld solar charger. "No dust, no wear and tear," Nate said. "This is brand spanking new. Whoever it is came from a time close to us and, like us, they haven't been here long. If they were part of the Genesis group, this would look older."

"If they aren't Genesis, they have to be from the ARCs, right?" Finch furrowed his brow. "I mean...who else could it be?"

PART TWO: LOLA

THREE

Tucker Freeman was not the original. He was the third. His grandfather and father were both Tucker Freeman, but all three men were different. His grandfather owned a farm in the Dakotas, and it was one of the only farms in the area that hadn't been sold to the government. He was a farmer. A no-nonsense man who focused on his work. Tucker's father hadn't wanted to be a farmer, he dreamed of bigger and better things, but his fast and furious lifestyle brought his life to an end by way of a car accident when Tucker was nine years old.

Tucker and his sister went to live with his grandparents. He loved them and saw nothing wrong with farming. In fact, Tucker thought his grandfather's farm was cool. And just at the end of the property, lit up like a stadium for the Super Bowl, was the construction site for one of the ARCs.

When they first started building it Tucker didn't live with his grandfather, and he recalled that they all believed it was going to be a mall.

It wasn't long before they realized what it was and suddenly it was exciting.

Tucker remembered the day he moved in with his grandparents. It was the day before the Omni-4 took off to go through the Androski to check out the Noah, or the new Earth.

At that young age, Tucker's world stopped. Everywhere else was suffering disasters, but his world, with the loss of his parents, collapsed.

He found a strange and obsessive focus on the Omni mission. He watched every bit of news, every social media video. Stories of the crew's lives, what they would do. When he wanted to cry and get angry, he looked to the Omni and the hope they sought.

A CGI generated animation speculated about their entire mission through the wormhole. When he missed his parents, he watched that video. The animated likeness of the teacher reminded him of his mother, and 'The Clutch' looked exactly like his dad. Acted like him, too. He was dashing, personable. He imagined his parents were on board the Omni. That they didn't die at all, they went on a mission.

When the news reported the Omni didn't return as scheduled, everyone was sad. But not Tucker. He knew they weren't dead, that there hadn't been an accident, but they had found a home and just like that old satellite, were having a hard time getting back.

They would return, he believed, eventually.

Until then he looked to the sky, did his homework, and watched more omni videos; someone turned that one mission animation into a short video series.

In one episode they landed, in another they faced trouble, and in the finale they encountered friendly alien life.

It was fiction, though not in Tucker's mind.

Now, as he stared at the recent colonist rejection notice, Tucker thought back to a conversation he'd had with his grandfather one night while watching the ARC's construction. It was nearly three years after the Omni had left Earth.

"Do you think I'll get on that ARC, Pap?" Tucker asked.

"Well," his grandfather exhaled. "You see that ARC there won't go up for at least another fifty years. That's a long time. Now mind you, I think you'll be plenty healthy but fifty-nine isn't young. I reckon they're gonna want younger people on that ARC. Not saying you won't get picked. You just never know."

"I want to go up there," Tucker said looking up to the sky. "I want to be like the crew of Omni-4."

"You know they never came back."

"There's still time," Tucker said.

"That's a good answer." His grandfather patted Tucker's knee. "That's optimism."

"Then I'm gonna be positive I will go up there."

"You're a pretty smart fella," his grandfather said. "Maybe if you come up with something really big and really important, something they need, then maybe they'll have no choice but to ask you along."

"Yeah, I can do that. I'm smart," Tucker said. "I'll invent something. But I'm staying right here to do it."

His grandfather laughed a little. "Not much inventing for science can be done here in North Dakota. Got to go to a good college, too."

Tucker shook his head. "This is one of the safest places on Earth. I need to stay here so I can make sure nothing happens to my invention."

His grandfather furrowed his brow. "Why do you say that?"

"Because of that, Pap." Tucker pointed to the ARC. "That is to save humanity. To stop man from going extinct. To move them elsewhere."

"Correct."

"Well, would they build the hope for mankind in a place it could be destroyed?"

His grandfather looked at him. "Forget what I said about you being pretty smart. You're more than that. You really are. I believe you will come up with that invention."

"Now if I could just figure out what it would be."

"Want my suggestion?" his grandfather asked.

Tucker nodded.

His grandfather pointed to the ARC. "Figure out a way to get that thing off the ground. You do that...you'll have a seat."

Tucker's grandfather wasn't doing that family thing, pumping sunshine into Tucker, overly stating how smart he was. His grandfather didn't need to because Tucker *was* smart. In fact, he was a genius. Always ahead in school, graduating at fifteen.

But as astute as he was, Tucker was grounded. He didn't act like a scholar; he was a home-grown farm boy. He acted it and talked like it.

In his mind, his entire life boiled down to getting the ARC off the ground. He knew from news stories and articles that was holding it up.

It was his mission.

One he didn't want to fail, but he did.

As smart as Tucker was, as technologically and scientifically inclined as he seemed to be, he wasn't able to figure out the propulsion problem of the ARC. He tried, but it was above him and he wasn't able to grasp what would make it work. So he focused on what he knew: growing and farming.

He was, however, able to figure out a way to have a sustainable farming system that would not take up too much room or weight on the ARC. It was to be utilized immediately in case for some reason the ARCS weren't able to land.

He was praised, even awarded, because he was only twenty-two when he patented his invention. From there he joined the air force search and rescue, but worked mainly in agriculture, salvaging areas hit by disasters.

From inventing for space to inventing on the ground, his next breakthrough was the biggest yet: the floating farm system. The Sharm.

The Department of Navy proudly announced as much on Tucker's twenty-seventh birthday.

The prototype set sail three years later.

He only wished his grandfather had been alive to see it.

Sadly he had passed one year before the announcement. At least Tucker was able to share his idea with the man who had influenced his life the most. He'd received his expert feedback as he designed it.

With rising oceans, seaboard cities disappeared, and farming land was hit hard by earthquakes, floods, and other ravaging natural disasters.

The world was starving.

Food was scarce and rationed.

The way things were going, most of the human race stood a chance of starving before the ARCs even lifted from the ground.

His invention was a floating farm the size of a five-hundred-foot aircraft carrier. In fact, they reconditioned an old carrier for the prototype. Staffed with a skeleton farming, harvest, and ship crew, the farming system was a hydroponic growth system which utilized a desalination system aboard each floating farm.

The Chinese had been creating an ARC that not only would lift off the ground and make it through space, but would float once it landed on the new planet. The US Navy immediately started to reconfigure their designs.

It was brilliant, he was told.

Not only did he solve a huge food shortage problem on Earth, he may have potentially solved one on the new planet, which was close to seventy percent water.

So with all that accomplishment at such a young age, why did he get rejected as a colonist?

Tucker had done everything he was supposed to do.

Everything to get on the Genesis and be part of their colonist mission.

Each step was preplanned. He applied and was accepted to the Space Corps, he did his training there. Then he went through their rigorous process of applying to be a colonist or crew member.

Tucker believed he had every qualification. He was trained, and having lost his grandfather, and then his sister to the Seattle Quake, he had no family attachments on Earth. Plus, he'd invented the Sharm. He made it to the final selection process and was confident he would be one of the two dozen crew or one of the hundred colonists. Maybe he had been too confident, because he felt blindsided when he got the letter.

He excitedly opened it, thinking it was his orders. After all, they were waiting until three weeks before takeoff to announce the colonists.

But he knew when he read the opening line, "We regret to inform you…"

He felt as if he had been hit with a ton of bricks.

The final paragraph was a small consolation. It stated because of his achievements and contributions to the continuity of humanity he was assured a place on one of the ARCs. Tucker didn't want to wait another twenty-five years, he wanted to go now.

There were private expeditions, some would probably face disaster before even leaving the atmosphere, but

Tucker didn't try to get on one of those, he had placed all his eggs in one basket with Genesis one and two. There wasn't even time to apply for one of the private ones anymore.

He felt defeated. His entire life's goal, all that he'd done, worked for, was to get on the next mission out, and it didn't happen.

Tucker was about to quit it all, just go back to the farm, screw it, then the phone call came.

"Captain Freeman?" a British laced voice spoke on the other end. "My name is William Marshman, I am the director of the European Space Agency. We were just informed you didn't make the cut for the Genesis twin ships."

"Wow," Tucker said. "I just got the letter. You guys are good."

"We asked to be informed," Marshman said. "You're a vital part of the future."

"Yeah, well, unfortunately not vital enough to be on the Genesis."

"Their loss is our gain. I have a proposition for you."

"I didn't think the ESA was doing a Noah mission."

"We're not. It's a government and civilian effort involving several countries. Are you interested in hearing what I have to say?"

"Does it involve me going through the Androski this cycle?"

"Without a doubt."

Even though Marshman couldn't see it Tucker grinned, and in the same breath turned on his professional side. "Mr. Marshman...I'm all ears."

FOUR

Paradise, WV

Decades earlier, it been the training facility and launch site for Omni-4. The site had been chosen because it never experienced any of the natural disasters that plagued the nation. Even after all those years, the facility was untouched by nature's fury and then became the site for the Genesis Mission.

Joshua Quinn was proud to be there. It was an honor to be on the same ground as the crew of the Omni-4. Their pictures graced the entrance hallway of the main building. He felt their presence, their bravery, and he took from that.

He was also proud to be not only part of the Genesis Mission, but commander of both of the vessels that would take colonists, crew, and supplies to the Noah, the second Earth.

It had been a long, hard journey to get that position and it was one he wasn't going to take for granted.

He also didn't take for granted Tom Waite.

Tom was a vat of knowledge and one of the most respected individuals that Quinn knew. Tom was a man in his forties when he led the Omni-4 mission and watched it take off. Now he was pushing retirement, but he was still a strong figure.

Tom was the head of it all. He once told Quinn that it felt very personal to him. Because he knew those who were on board the Omni. That was the day, two years earlier, when Quinn had arrived at Paradise, newly named as commander of the mission. Before he had a crew or even passengers. But he'd had one thing. A sealed silver case that Tom had been holding onto for decades. It was something that he handed over to Quinn to take care of personally. It was for the crew of the Omni-4, when, not if, Quinn met them on the new planet. Tom was certain they'd arrived, were safe, and were just never able to return home.

"So we'll be moving the colonists into Buildings A and B," Tom said as he and Quinn walked the main road of the complex. "They start arriving tomorrow for training."

"You think three weeks is enough?" Quinn asked.

"We had Reyanne Harper trained in two. She had no experience. These colonists have a lot." He handed Quinn a computer tablet. "Take a look."

"I'm glad this wasn't my decision," Quinn said as he swiped through.

"I had very little influence, if you can believe it."

"No, not really." Quinn paused in swiping, then he moved his hand up and down. "He's not here. Did he turn it down? I thought for sure he wanted to go."

"Who?"

"Tucker Freeman." Quinn handed the tablet back to Tom. "Or did I miss him?"

"You didn't miss him. He's not on here. He wasn't selected."

Quinn stopped walking. "Are you kidding me? He's a good man, prime candidate. He's a genius, no he's an agricultural genius. These people really, some of them don't even compare. What the hell, Tom? I got it when he wasn't named crew. I figured you didn't want him busy with that, but not a colonist? That makes absolutely no sense to me."

"No, it doesn't," Tom replied. "But there are reasons. Freeman is a problem solver. He has this amazing mind. He will be guaranteed a place on the ARC. Yes, he would be a tremendous asset on Noah, but right now, Earth still needs him."

With a disgruntled "hmm," Quinn peered up to the sky and to the small planet that could be seen in the daylight. It looked like a huge, bright star. "On the ARC, huh? At the rate that thing is coming at us" — he looked at Tom — "is Earth going to be around in twenty-five years?"

FIVE

Japan Aerospace Exploration Agency (JAXA)

Chofu City, Tokyo

Within three days of the phone call from Marshman, Tucker had traveled to Dallas via coach on a budget airline, only to board a private jet when he arrived. Although, with the constant earthquake activity in Texas, Tucker was surprised that was even a destination.

Dallas was the last of the remaining large metropolises still intact. Most of the others had been destroyed by earthquakes or buried under water that failed to recede back into the Gulf of Mexico.

He imagined years earlier it must have been a shock for those who remembered the glory days pre-disaster. Now it was commonplace.

He didn't get to experience any tremors, though he was warned he would. In a twisted way, experiencing one would have been fun.

Tucker didn't even know where he was going. All he'd been told was to pack a bag; he wasn't returning home.

There was a lot of life going into his one bag, but he did it.

Before he left, he visited the memorial site of his sister and the grave of his grandfather, both of which were located on the old farm property. Land that was eventually acquired from his grandfather to stop spectators from watching the ARC like a tourist attraction.

They allowed his grandfather to live there until he passed. They didn't tear down the house. Workers actually lived there, and small trailers were set up on the property.

Tucker was a celebrity of sorts to those in the ARC world, so they had no problem with him visiting the grave.

He said his goodbyes, telling his grandfather, "I'm doing it, Pap, I'm going up there," before leaving the farm for the final time.

He napped on the private plane, as advised by the pilot because it was going to be a long flight. He didn't expect to land in Japan. He was informed by the flight crew that he wasn't to get too comfortable as they would be leaving again in a day. They were picking up another crew member, then they'd head to their final destination.

"Which is?" Tucker asked.

"We really can't say."

A driver waited for him at the airport. Tucker managed to get a call through to Marshman while in the car.

Marshman had been sleeping and answered with a groggy, "Hello."

"What the heck?" Tucker greeted him over the phone. "I'm halfway across the world and no one will tell me anything."

"I apologize for that. I truly do. We just need to be secretive until we are secure at the facility."

"And that is where?"

"You'll know when you get here."

"It's that secret?" Tucker asked.

"It's that important."

"Okay, I'll refrain from asking anymore."

"Thank you. I am going back to bed. I will see you tomorrow at the facility."

Tucker ended the call, placed the phone in his pocket, and stared out the window. He would have loved to have seen Tokyo before the world went on rationed living. Restaurants were all a thing of the past. The buildings remained but they were empty and dark. Bars and drinking establishments stayed; occasionally there was food, but not often.

The days of frivolous eating, wasting portions, and overstocked grocery stores had disappeared five years earlier. That was a shame. The young generation would never know it, just like they wouldn't know JAXA in its heyday.

Tucker had been there once, twenty years earlier. It was like the pictures of Kennedy Space Center when it was still above water. As they pulled into the grounds of JAXA, Tucker barely recognized it.

The grounds were barren, the grass dried, and some of the bushes and trees grew out of control. Even the driveway lacked maintenance. The rocket and part space shuttle that graced the outside of the building were weather worn. The front of the building appeared abandoned; the windows hadn't been washed in years. The parking lot had one lone car.

"Holy crap," Tucker said, "is there anyone even here? Or is that a question you can't handle?"

"I found it strange that I was to bring you here. This facility has been closed for years. I think it is used for storage. I'm not sure."

"And you're supposed to just leave me here."

"I guess that car"—the driver pointed—"is the person you are meeting."

"Do you have a name?"

"Me? I'm Len."

"No, not you, but nice to meet you, Len. A name for the person I am meeting."

Len shook his head.

"Oh, well. Thank you for the ride." Tucker grabbed his bag, stepped out, and closed the door. "Oh, one more..." Before he could finish, Len had driven away. Tucker tossed up his hand. "Great." He shouldered his bag and walked to the main front doors.

They were open.

Thinking a sarcastic, *Wow, security is top notch* he walked inside.

The entire front lobby was empty except the visitor's desk. There were no chairs, no displays.

Tucker would have thought it was a joke of some kind, being dropped off in a totally empty building in a strange country, had it not been for the one car in the parking lot. That told him that someone was there, unless it was an elaborate practical joke.

He was about to call out when he heard his name.

"Captain Tucker Freeman?"

"Um, yeah," he replied, looking around.

"Sorry I wasn't down there to greet you," the male voice said, then was followed by the sounds of footsteps.

Tucker looked to his right and saw an Asian man in a JAXA jumpsuit coming down the open staircase. He held what looked like a metal suitcase and moved in a quick, upbeat pace.

The man extended his hand to Tucker. "Samu Horato, you can call me Sam," he introduced himself. "It's a pleasure to meet you. My car is right out front. I told Marshman you could stay with me until we leave tomorrow for the base. Unless you'd feel more comfortable at a hotel."

"No, no. Not at all. That's fine," Tucker said. "I'm comfortable anywhere. So why did we meet here?"

"I guess I could have met you elsewhere," Sam said. "But this was nostalgia. Part of history, you know."

Tucker nodded.

"And I had to get information, some files."

Tucker balked a little and gave a quirky smile. "There's no security here. I'm surprised they left anything behind."

"They didn't think anything of this." He tapped the case. "It's data. Old data."

"Old data?" Tucker asked. "How old?"

"Like last century, the nineties."

Tucker whistled. "Yeah, that's a little old. Though I can't imagine what data from 1990 would be useful now."

Sam winked. "You'd be surprised. "

"So are you the computer guy on this mission?" Tucker asked.

"No, I'm the engineer. I actually designed the craft for the Robinson Mission."

"The Robinson Mission?" Tucker asked. "Is that what it's called?"

"It is."

"I wonder why."

Sam shrugged. "I didn't name the mission, they did. I did name the ship though. It's called The Lola."

"That's an odd name for a ship."

"It's a cool name."

"It's also pretty impressive," Tucker said. "Really. You designed the ship for this mission."

"No, I designed the ship, the mission found me. Just like they found you. My accomplishments and theories. Which you will hear about tomorrow. But I think the ship is nothing compared to the Sharm. Now that's impressive."

"Thanks."

"You had to have made a bundle from that. How rich did it make you?"

"Rich?" Tucker said confused. "Was I supposed to make money from it?"

Sam chuckled. "That's funny."

"I wasn't joking."

The smile dropped from Sam's face. "For real?"

"Yeah, it's a humanity thing. Who makes money from saving humanity?"

Sam started walking toward the door.

"Wait," Tucker said. "Did you make money from the Lola design?"

"I made a ton of money. But that doesn't matter now, does it? Let's head out. We have an early flight tomorrow." He pushed open the door.

"Where are we going?" Tucker asked. "Or aren't you at liberty to say?"

"I'm not at liberty to say, but I'll tell you anyhow. The base is located in the balmy paradise of Siberia."

That made Tucker laugh. "Okay, then don't tell me." He shook his head and followed Sam out. He figured that was Sam's way of pacifying him, or telling a joke. After all, there was no such thing as the balmy paradise of Siberia.

SIX

Siberia

Tucker really felt that Sam was perpetuating the joke when he kept saying, "The parka is a bit much."

Tucker smiled and thought how Sam must have really taken him for some country bumpkin. Anyone with a right mind would know that a parka was needed in Siberia.

He had gotten to know Sam some the night before. They drank and talked. Sam was only a few years older than Tucker and Tucker envied him. He smiled and remained jovial even with his tragic life.

"I was so excited," Sam had told him. "My first mission up there was exploratory, basic, every space agency was doing them." He pointed up as they sat on his balcony. "I went, only to come home and find an earthquake had wiped out our village. My wife, two kids, parents, everyone...gone. I wanted to go up there and never come back."

"Now you are," Tucker told him.

"Now I am. But I will tell you. I can't wait to get back to Siberia. I was there two months ago, it was beautiful. If it wasn't space, I'd go there and live. You don't need a coat."

What a jokester, Tucker thought.

Until, of course, he arrived.

Suddenly, Tucker looked like a fool for not only carrying that coat but wearing a heavy sweatshirt.

It was warm, balmy, and more than that, it was green.

Marshman was there to greet them when they stepped off the private plane. He was a smaller man, balding with glasses. He extended his hand offering a warm handshake. "Didn't Sam tell you about the weather?" He nodded to the coat Tucker carried.

"Yeah, but I thought he was joking. It's Siberia. When did things change?"

"About six months ago," Marshman replied. "Didn't you know?"

"I'm sorry I was bull balls deep in preparing to get selected for the Genesis, which I didn't," Tucker said.

"But we have you and couldn't be happier," Marshman told him.

"What exactly is this mission?" Tucker asked. "I'm here, so I guess you can tell me."

"Yes, yes, I can," Marshman replied. "Let's get your things inside, and I'll explain."

"Meet Lola," Marshman said as they approached what looked like an airfield and the craft, Lola.

Tucker didn't need to ask if it was solar charged. Usually on the ships the solar panels retracted, but these covered the top of the tubular-shaped object which looked like a jumbo jet that had been cut in half, rather than something that would be ejected into space.

While it was shorter than a plane, it was wider. The wheels kept it closer to the ground than Tucker had ever seen.

34

"Okay...why is it so low?" Tucker asked.

Sam explained, "After everyone boards and the engines start, it'll lift."

Tucker nodded. "And how is this thing gonna get up there?"

"My designed propulsion system. It didn't work for the ARCs, but this, it works like a beaut. She's been up there four times. You know, just some test runs. But she takes off like a jet."

"Enough power to punch through the atmosphere?" Tucker asked.

Sam nodded. "Like the movies they used to make."

Tucker whistled. "Well, this is impressive. Why here? Why Siberia?"

Marshman answered, "Global position, secrecy. We've been working on the Robinson for nine years."

"What kind of mission is it?" Tucker asked.

"Like the Genesis, a colonist mission. It's pretty much a one-way ticket, Captain Freeman," Marshman said. "This is mainly a privately funded project."

"You said different countries," Tucker said.

"That's true. Japan..." Marshman pointed to Sam. "The other three, Russia, the UK, and Germany, because they built this bad boy." He cleared his throat. "Sorry. Girl."

"The UK, meaning you?" Tucker asked. "Will you be going along?"

Marshman shook his head. "No, not me. I'm your control down here. Plus, I have too much family and I think I need to see what happens to the world."

"Now, I am not a continuity of mankind expert," Tucker said, "but how are we gonna colonize with five people? Unless you're just wanting to set up farming and technology for when the ARCs arrive."

"Yes. In a sense," Marshman explained. "As you know the Genesis selection process was precise. Those selected, even the crew, had to have a specific skill set needed to set in place a long-term survival plan. A new world. They also agreed to be paired off with a procreation partner, how that will end up working out..." Marshman shrugged. "Who knows."

"This is much smaller," Tucker said. "So we aren't carrying fifty people like Genesis one and two."

Marshman shook his head. "No, we are not. We are carrying five crew and seventeen civilians."

That answer took Tucker by surprise. "Civilians?"

"Much like the pilgrims did centuries ago. I said this is publicly funded. Money doesn't mean much anymore, it doesn't buy much except existence. Four families funded seventy-five percent of the mission. Each of these families gave every penny they had to survive and live on."

Sam clarified, "Families with children."

Tucker's jaw dropped some. "There are children on this flight? Small children?" When he received confirmation, he shook his head with a chuckle. "I get it now. The Robinson. That's why you named it the Robinson."

Sam looked at him curiously.

"The Robinsons," Tucker explained. "*Lost in Space*. It was a television show. One of the few they played after new network programing stopped."

Sam shook his head.

"*Lost in Space*. The Robinsons were a family chosen to go live on another planet. In the remake it was because Earth was dying. *Lost in Space* Robinsons, Robinson Crusoe, swiss family Robinson. There's a common element where a Robinson is stranded somewhere and has to survive. I'm looking at you and you are lost."

"I am," Sam said.

"I'll explain later, however..." Tucker faced Marshman. "Do these people realize the risk? I mean if we have to turn around and come back, they'll have nothing. We don't even know if this planet Noah is habitable."

"We believe we do," Marshman said.

"How?" Tucker asked. "I mean we can speculate with pictures. But Omni-4 never returned. We don't know."

"Actually," Sam said, "we do. Follow me."

Sam turned and walked from the airfield.

The control room didn't look much more than a small computer room, with a tracking and radar screen no bigger than four foot wide.

There was one man who sat at the control counter, facing the computer.

Maybe they were on skeleton crew until liftoff.

Tucker hoped.

Marshman introduced Tucker to Ray, the other engineer that would be seeing the flight off.

"Pull up project NAT," Marshman told Ray.

"What is project NAT?" Tucker asked.

Marshman pointed to Sam.

"Project Needle and Thread," Sam answered.

"Another one of yours?" Tucker questioned.

"Well, the redesign is," Sam answered.

"NASA has their own version of Needle and Thread. But I can bet NASA doesn't have a Sam or his changes," Marshman said.

"Or," Sam added, "our information."

"You don't share?" Tucker asked.

Marshman shook his head. "They refuse to acknowledge what we are doing as viable, so we won't share our information."

"Which is?"

"Everybody has put a probe through the Androski, it would be stupid not to," Sam said. "But the probes weren't coming back and transmitting any information. Then we attached a line to one."

"That's pretty brilliant," Tucker said.

Marshman nodded. "It is and we did share that info. We were able to send the prob though and pull it back."

"But the problem," Sam said, "was the only data we got, which we assume NASA received as well, was that there was some sort of power loss going through."

"So it was pretty much dead when you pulled it back?" Tucker questioned.

"Yes," Sam answered. "Then I did the readings and re-designed it two weeks ago. It was rigged together quickly because we just didn't have enough of a window when the wormhole would be open to build a whole new one. Basically, I did my own version of a faraday cage, and it worked."

Tucker's eyes widened. "It went though and collected data."

Sam nodded. "Yes, and that data will protect us. See, NASA knows there was a power loss going through, they have to. If they know that then they know Omni probably lost power for about fourteen to fifteen seconds."

"Not enough to kill them, but enough to knock 'em out," Tucker said. "Not kill them."

"We hope. Now..." Sam indicated to Ray to start the video. "This is all we have of the NAT going through."

Tucker watched the flashes of light, then it went black. But there was only a brief second of power loss then distorted images appeared. It looked as if a camera was extremely out of focus.

"Is that the other side?" Tucker asked.

"It is," Marshman added. "We have photos that an expert has worked on. They are a little clearer. Ray, can you pull them up."

A blurry, yet distinguishable enough image appeared. It was of a blue planet. "That's not the Noah," Tucker said.

"No, it's not, that's a moon of sorts," Marshman said.

"Tucker, Einstein theorized that wormholes weren't a portal to another galaxy, but rather," Sam said, "to another time."

"Time travel?" Tucker chuckled. "Another time?"

Marshman said, "You commented that we didn't know for sure that the Noah was habitable."

"We don't," Tucker said.

"We do." Marshman pointed to the screen. "It is." Another planet appeared on the screen. "We know for sure it's habitable. This isn't another galaxy or universe, and that isn't some planet we named Earth Two. It's the future; we don't know when or how far, but we do know that…is Earth."

It was a lot to take in.

Tucker retreated to his quarters with copies of the images. He stared at them, analyzing them closely. Wondering if they were right, that it was Earth. They were blurry and pixelized.

He thought of his conversation with Sam right after the control room meeting.

Sam's words burned in his mind. "Our geo guy looked at these. They look similar, but they aren't. Each time we sent NAT through, the earth changed."

"He can't be sure. I mean they are still really blurry," Tucker said.

"True. But I'm guessing he's right."

Sam pointed out what he had been told, the shift of the continents and oceans.

"If he is right," Tucker said, "and you're right, then there's no guarantee when we'll end up."

"Nope. We just have to hope it's long enough after Planet X locks into rotation that things are settled and the disasters have stopped."

To Tucker it just seemed to be science fiction. Time travel wasn't really possible and if it was, would they have the ability to physically hold proof of the future by way of shoddy probe images?

Do the passengers know? Tucker wondered.

Marshman told him they didn't and there was no reason to tell them until they landed.

Whatever time they arrived, as long as it was safer than what they faced now, they were getting what they paid for: a chance at a longer life.

Tucker still didn't know much about the mission. He hadn't met the families or even knew anything about them, the only crew member he'd met was Sam.

Tucker hadn't even found out what his role was specifically.

He guessed he would in the days to come. He knew they were leaving soon and wanted to focus on something, because any idle time meant time he spent wrestling with a moral dilemma.

They had the knowledge, near proof that they weren't going to another planet, but rather another time, and they didn't share that with anyone.

Genesis was going in lacking vital information.

Part of a commander's job is to be educated and know everything there is to know so he or she can plan on possible outcomes.

Or maybe they did know and just weren't sharing it with Marshman.

The only way for Tucker to find out was to reach out to Quinn, the commander of the Genesis.

Unfortunately, there was no way to do that. All that Tucker could do was learn his job, get ready for the mission, and possibly convince Marshman to share the information.

After all, it wasn't a competition. It was a race to space, it was an attempt to save the human race, even just the tiniest fraction.

They all shared a common goal, they needed to share information as well.

SEVEN

Paradise, WV

Quinn had just settled in for the evening when he was summonsed to speak to Waites. He welcomed the diversion as he was certain he wouldn't be able to sleep at all. Quinn, like everyone else on board the Genesis, had been assigned a procreation partner. Something every single one of them had to agree to.

A partner for life, to create life on the new Earth.

Quinn was all for it, until he met his chosen partner; he had no say in the matter. Scientific means of compatibility put them together and Quinn was certain the science was off.

Her name was Dana and she wasn't very nice. Quinn was never one to care about looks, after all, looks fade, personalities didn't.

He hoped hers would one day.

She was attractive, but tough. She came across as crass, edgy, and probably could beat any man Quinn knew in an arm-wrestling match. Not that her arms were big, he just happened to see her lift a case with ease.

Dana was a systems analysist on board. She also had a lot of responsibility with the cargo. Quinn wanted to meet her, introduce himself, maybe even get a chuckle with her about the 'arranged relationship' but she wasn't having it.

In fact...

"What do you want, Commandeer Quinn?"

"Well, you're not busy," Quinn said. "I thought I would get to know you."

"You don't think we'll have time for that when we land? Trust me, we'll have time for that."

"Are you misunderstanding me?" Quinn asked. "Maybe you got the wrong idea."

"I don't think so. I'm your procreation partner."

"No, no." Quinn nervously waved his hand out. "I wasn't here to bring that up, well, I was, but not in the way I believe you're thinking."

"There's no other way to think. I am your life partner for bearing children. I don't need to be your friend."

"I kind of think that might help," Quinn said.

Dana shook her head. "It won't, because I don't care."

"If you didn't want to do this, why are you?" Quinn asked.

"I want to go up there." She pointed up. "I have since I was a little girl."

"We all have."

"I'll do what I need to do to make it happen. I also feel I spoke for a lot of women when I said, 'I don't have to like it to know my responsibility lies with starting the human race up there.'"

"I'm sure a lot of men aren't happy about it either."

Dana laughed and walked away.

"Okay..." Quinn stood by himself for a moment, baffled at her attitude. He supposed he'd question all night long if the rest of his personal life on the new planet was going to be a miserable existence.

That was when he was called to meet Waites.

Strangely he wasn't called to the control room, or Waites's office. He met him in the cafeteria.

It was closed and empty, the only lights on were those on the vending machine and the small round ones above the serving line.

"What's going on?" Quinn asked.

Waites sat at a table alone, a folder next to a bowl of cereal. "Sit down, Quinn."

Quinn slid down across from him.

"You're right. Or were right," Waites said.

"What do you mean?"

"About Tucker Freeman. You're right, it is a mistake that he is not on this mission."

With an exhale of relief, Quinn sat back. "Does this mean he's in?"

"I've made call after call these last couple days," Waites said. "I finally got the program to see the light on Freeman. That he is essential to the startup there. He's needed in more ways than one."

"That's what I was saying. They made a grave error rejecting him."

"They understand that, saw the error of their ways. One of their big arguments was that he wouldn't have a pairing. He would be the odd man out, so to speak."

"Oh, hell, he can have mine. I can spend the rest of my life alone. Trust me, I met her."

Waites let out a chuckle. "Well, unfortunately...we reached out to Freeman. No answer. In fact, his phone went straight to voice mail. But we weren't giving up."

"Weren't?" Quinn asked. "As if you have?'

"We have no choice. We went to the farm. All the workers on the ARC know him. They told us he was leaving. We did a little more digging." Waites pushed the folder to Quinn.

44

Quinn apprehensively opened it and read. His eyes shifted back and forth. "Are you kidding me?"

"All there."

"He's been picked up for a privately funded colony ship."

"Yes."

"You have to stop him," Quinn said. "You know and I know, every expert is saying those private ships aren't built to withstand the Androski."

"This one may," Waites said.

"You mean to tell me the genius who could keep the world alive, one of the smartest men on the planet, will float out into space on a private ship that will more than likely crumble in the wormhole."

"We hope not. Just wanted to let you know. We're gonna keep trying though," Waites said. "We will find him and talk to him."

"I can't blame you. But this shouldn't be a situation. Tucker Freeman should have been a given." He pushed the folder back to Waites.

It was frustrating. Quinn hoped they would be able to convince Tucker to join Genesis. If not, he could only hope that all would go well and he'd meet up with Tucker on the new planet.

EIGHT

Siberia

There was an old saying, 'If you want something done right, you do it yourself.'

It was one carried through generations, and one Quinn subscribed to.

When the location of Tucker Freeman was discovered and they realized it was out of range of normal communications, Quinn didn't trust any official from NASA to convince Tucker to join Genesis. He had to be the one. He was commander of the mission, and he hoped that when Tucker met him, he not only would be impressed at the efforts made but accepting of the apology for the error.

Of course, Quinn had no idea what exactly traveling to Siberia entailed.

It took days and a recent rash of hurricanes didn't help. He was glad he dressed appropriately. In his lifetime, Siberia was always cold. Not in a perpetual state of spring like it was now.

He had never met Tucker Freeman. The only pictures he'd seen of the guy were when he was young and accepting awards. All dressed up in a suit that looked a little big.

Quinn knew Tucker was a man that came from modest means. He had heard stories about him, how he looked like the kind of country boy one would see wearing a backwards baseball cap, faded Levi jeans, a rock and roll tee-shirt from decades earlier, driving to the race car track and spitting chew into an empty beer bottle.

Quinn always thought that was an exaggeration until he arrived at the secret Siberian base. He was greeted by a man named Marshman who led him to a hanger. Marshman pointed to a solar buggy. The man behind the wheel was Asian and wearing what looked like an astronaut jumpsuit. Leaning over the front end of the buggy, wearing jeans and a tee-shirt, was the man Quinn assumed was Tucker.

He was everything everyone described with the exception of the beer bottle spittoon.

"Try it now," the man with the thick country accent told the driver.

The driver started the buggy. "You did it. How is that possible when I'm the mechanical genius?"

"You didn't design this. It was too simple. Got a wire loose, that's all."

"He," Marshman said, "is Tucker and the man you're looking for."

"Fixing solar buggies?" Quinn asked.

"Everyone is hands on here," Marshman said. "We don't have crews to change a bolt or screw in a lightbulb."

"I see that. So, I assume people aren't on vacation."

"Hardly." He led Quinn closer and called out, "Tucker, you have a visitor."

"I have a visitor in a top-secret facility way up in the middle of yonder?" Tucker looked over. "Holy Cow. I'll be. Look, Sam, it's Commander Joshua Quinn of the Genesis Project."

"Get the hell out of here," Sam replied.

"No joke. I know them all by sight." Tucker wiped off his hands, stuffed the towel in the back pocket of his jeans and walked hand extended to Quinn. "Sir, how are you?"

"Mr. Freeman, it is an honor to meet you," Quinn said.

"Please, call me Tucker. The honor's mine. Wow. You came all the way here...Aren't you supposed to be training to go in a couple weeks?"

"I've been training for years," Quinn replied. "This is part of my mission."

"I don't understand," Tucker said.

"Is there somewhere we can sit down and talk?" Quinn asked.

"Sure," Tucker answered.

Sam interjected, "Is it something that's confidential, because I'm curious as to why you came all the way up here from Paradise, West Virginia, and if I wait to hear from Tucker, I'm sure I'll get the short commercial version."

"It's up to Tucker," Quinn said.

"Well, considering I haven't a clue what you want, Sam can come. So can Mr. Marshman if he wants."

Marshman held up his hand. "I don't need to be there. I already know what he's here for."

"Oh, okay, well," Tucker said. "Sam and I will join you. Since this is a sit-down talk, let's go to the dining hall. I'm hungry, I can go for peanut butter sandwich. Sam?"

"I'll pass on the peanut butter and jam sandwich," Sam said. "I'll grab something else."

Tucker laughed. "Jam? Not jam. Jelly. Has to be jelly."

"What's the difference?"

"Oh, and they call me uncultured country." Tucker shook his head with a smile and led the way.

Instantly, Quinn liked him. With Tucker's brains and personality he just couldn't figure out why he was rejected in the first place.

Tucker wasn't joking about the peanut butter and jelly sandwich. The perfectly crafted sandwich, one he made himself, sat on a plate cut diagonally. Perched to the right of the plate was a tall glass of milk.

"You sure I can't make you one?" Tucker asked.

Quinn waved his hand. "Maybe later."

He took a drink of his milk and placed the glass down with a post-drink refreshing exhale. "Man, that's good. Still trying to figure out a way to get a cow on the ship."

Quinn laughed.

Sam shook his head. "He's not joking."

"Maybe a calf," Tucker said. "Can we get a calf? We're gonna need milk for the babies. Especially since the genesis is planning to pop them out."

"I told you before," Sam said, "there isn't enough time to put a chamber on the ship. Get used to the powder stuff."

"Well I won't like it." Tucker took a bite of his sandwich and washed it down. "What can I do for you, Mr. Quinn?"

"Tucker." Quinn folded his hands on the table and leaned forward. "On behalf of the United States government and NASA, I would like to extend our deepest regrets and apologies for not selecting you for the Genesis. It was unfair and I think that your rejection was purely political. Having you on Earth gives people nice feelings.'

"That's nice. But did you have something to do with the decision for me not to go?" Tucker asked.

"No."

"So why are you apologizing?"

"I wanted to be the one."

Tucker whistled. "Wow, you came all the way here to apologize. That was really nice. Not necessary…then again you can't call here."

"No, Tucker, I came all the way here with hopes to get you to grab your stuff, come with me, and be part of the Genesis."

"Really?" Tucker asked.

"Yes," Quinn answered.

"Question," Sam said. "All of you on the Genesis are paired off with procreation partners, how's that going to work for him?"

"I will give him mine."

Tucker laughed. "What's wrong with her?"

"Nothing."

"You're giving her up awfully fast."

"Okay, she's not nice."

"And you're stuck with her. I'm sure she's probably sore she's stuck with you and she's actually a nice person."

"What's wrong with me?" Quinn asked.

"Nothing that I know of." Tucker shrugged. "Maybe you aren't her type."

"Okay, okay. Obviously, a procreation partner isn't important to you," said Quinn. "So, can I take it you'll come back with me?"

Tucker groaned out and sat back. "I feel really bad."

"Why?" Quinn asked.

"You came all the way here and I am gonna have to say thank you and wow, how cool, but I also have to say no."

"Tucker, please, give this some thought. I am here until tomorrow morning. Think about it tonight. Sleep on it. Don't just say no right away," Quinn said. "This is a huge opportunity. They made a massive mistake when they didn't select you. I told them that. Hell, when I saw the manifest I got

50

mad and was shocked not to see your name. But you are needed."

"I am needed on this one. I already made a commitment to folks that wanted me on the mission from the get-go. They even gave me a title: Agricultural Geoengineer. It's a new thing. They made it for me. And they're pretty nice."

"Tucker," Sam said, "if you want to do this, please don't feel bad. This is something you dreamed of your entire adult life. Maybe you should take time to think about it."

"No, Sam, there is really nothing to think about," Tucker said. "Honest, this is where I stay."

"Tucker," Quinn spoke up, "you are a brilliant man. You have to realize the odds of success on these private missions are going to be slim. Most of these ships will crumble when they go through the Androski."

"Oh, we won't. I have faith in Sam's vision and ship," Tucker said. "I believe the odds will be in our favor. He built a good ship and thinks of things NASA does not."

"Like what?"

"Like attaching a line to the probe and sending it into the Androski so it comes right back," Tucker said.

"We did that," Quinn said. "That's how we learned about the power loss as you pass through. The probe was dead when it returned."

"Sam's wasn't."

"What?" Quinn looked at Sam. "How?"

"He fixed it."

Sam spoke with a lowered voice, "I'm really not so sure you were supposed to say anything."

"Oh, who cares. What's Marshman gonna do, kick me off the mission?" Tucker asked.

"True," said Sam. "But..."

"Did you see what's on the other side?" Quinn asked.

"We did."

"Tucker," Sam warned.

"Heck, Sam, what is it gonna hurt if we tell him what our probe saw?" Tucker asked. "This isn't a race to see who can conquer it first. It's a race to save humanity."

"It has nothing to do with secrecy or trying to be one up on information," Sam said. "It has everything to do with how big the news is and how it could affect the mission. People may back out."

"Whoa, whoa, you have me curious," Quinn said. "Is it bad?"

"No," Tucker said.

"Yes," Sam said at the same time.

"Doesn't it depend on how you look at it?" Tucker asked.

"You look at it one way," Sam replied. "I look at it one way, others may not."

"Enough," Quinn stated. "Well, why don't you tell me and I'll make the decision, as commander, if I tell others. Okay? Obviously, this is something I should know."

Sam looked at Tucker and nodded.

"You're right." Tucker stood.

"Where are you going?" Quinn asked.

"I have to run to my quarters and get something," Tucker told him. "Plus, I think you're gonna need that peanut butter sandwich."

Slowly, Quinn shuffled through the pixelated images. The folder was open on the table, with his sandwich next to it.

"This is unreal," Quinn said in shock. "I will say this actually crossed my mind."

"I think," Sam said, "it crossed all of our minds but it was too bizarre to admit."

"You said you sent the probe back in several times."

"Ten times we sent NAT through," Sam answered. "Each time was a...different time. It's hard to tell by the earth images, but you can see continent changes, unwanted changes, cloud coverings in this one"—Sam pulled an image forward indicating to the darker spot—"this is dust, lots of it. Some explosion, volcanic eruption. The distinct difference is Planet X."

Quinn nodded. "Apparently, Planet X hasn't settled into its new orbit in four of these time frames. Which leads me to believe..."

"They're in the past," Sam said. "It's nowhere to be seen. My guess is it's before 2015 when people started continuously seeing it in the sky. And by the images it looks a lot like Earth today. But X...it's nowhere."

"Past?" Quinn asked. "Or could it be so far in the future that it's gone?"

"It's past," said Sam.

"Jesus." Quinn sat back. "So there is a chance we can go through and end up back in the 1800s."

"Rare, slim," Sam stated. "I'm not an expert, but it's only ten percent."

"You can look at it this way," Tucker said. "We go through to the nineth century, park it somewhere and live. Isn't that what we're doing? Trying to save some inkling of the human race. Then again, you'd have to deal with the Civil War all over again. Heck, I'd aim for some place in South America."

"This doesn't worry you?" Quinn asked.

"No, it's a crap shoot," Tucker replied. "It's a chance we're all gonna take. Even though we're prepared for the power loss, we still could smash right into the new moon. Or Planet X."

"Certainly it's not as big as they're saying," Quinn stated.

"Big enough to kill us all," Sam said. "What are you going to do with the information?"

"Oh, I'm not saying a word," Quinn replied. "It is my judgement to keep this quiet. Like Tucker said, we're here to save them. Where or rather *when* we arrive isn't important, as long as we do. Just kind of throws a monkey wrench into getting things ready for the ARC."

"But hey," Tucker stated, "we have to go through under the assumption that we're making it better for whoever lands there. For all we know these four images may be fifty or a hundred years apart from each other, progressively. But I agree with your decision. I'd wait until you land."

Quinn nodded. "Thank you. And thank you for sharing this. It certainly gives me a heads-up. And"—he lifted his plate—"thanks for the sandwich."

Quinn returned to looking at the probe photos and discussing them with Tucker and Sam. A part of him hoped, somehow, someway, while he was in Siberia, he could get Tucker to change his mind. Even if he had to pull out the trump card that they had cows on Genesis Two.

Quinn spent the night learning about the Robinson mission, and in a way he envied them. They didn't have the regulations and rules that Genesis did. It seemed more relaxed— a pilgrimage to a new world. Only it wasn't new. While he didn't expect Marshman or Tucker to believe him, Quinn would keep everything he learned a secret. But he would use that knowledge.

54

His chopper was due to arrive late the next morning, giving Quinn time to see the ship, to learn about the Lola. A part of him didn't want to go. He wanted to stay but that wasn't an option. Like Tucker he'd made a commitment.

Tucker walked with him to the landing field where his helicopter waited.

He stopped a short distance from it to say goodbye, far enough away so the blade noise wouldn't drown him out.

"I have to say, Tucker, this has been a true pleasure."

"Thank you," Tucker replied. "I have read so much about you, I felt I knew you."

"Yeah, but you have read a lot about every astronaut going up there."

"I have. I really wanted to be a part."

"And now you are," Quinn said. "I only wish I could have somehow persuaded you to come back with me. We will really need you and no one can compare."

"That's very nice of you to say," Tucker replied. "And I'll tell you"—he leaned into Quinn—"that cow was awfully tempting."

"Yeah, I played the trump card."

"I have a feeling we'll meet again," Tucker said. "Either you'll be waiting for us or we will be waiting for you."

"Let's hope."

"You have that peanut butter and jelly sandwich I made for your trip?"

Quinn patted his bag. "All ready to eat on the flight. You make a good one."

"It's all in the bread," Tucker replied. "Good thing I know how to make it and we have enough supplies for me to make it."

"Without an oven?"

"Did the Pilgrims need an oven?"

"Yeah, they just made one," Quinn said.

"True."

"Well, my new friend." Quinn extended his hand. "Be safe."

"You as well." Tucker shook his hand.

"I'll see you on the other side," Quinn said, then he backed up and turned. He walked to the helicopter, crouching down as he neared it. Before stepping inside, he looked back. Tucker stood there watching. He waved once more to Tucker before getting on board.

Something inside of Quinn told him it wasn't goodbye, that somehow, some way they would meet up again.

At least he hoped.

Tucker Freeman would be a good one to have around when they landed on the Noah, or rather, as he'd just learned, Earth in the future.

But to Quinn, it might as well be a new world, because judging by what he'd seen, it was not the same. Nor would it ever be.

NINE

It was time.

There was a buzz in the air for launch day. The final checks had been made, everything was in order and it was just a matter of time. Tucker couldn't believe, with just under five hours' flight time to the Androski, they would be on the other side in under eight hours.

As he walked around the base, he thought of the old days of flight. How the astronauts needed hours to prepare for liftoff. Systems checks, suits checked, life-support systems, and each astronaut being secured in.

It wasn't like that now.

Technology had advanced.

It took no more time to prepare than it did for a domestic flight from one city to another.

They were almost ready to go.

Tucker double-checked the cargo and made sure he had what he needed in his personal bag. He would go back and check things one more time before they sealed the hatch.

On his return to the hanger before heading to the craft, he could see the families waiting to go. Watching as their belongings, limited to one bag and box each, were loaded

57

onto the ship. Tucker wished he had gotten a chance to meet them and to know them, but they'd been hidden away beforehand.

He would have time to learn who they were once they arrived. After all, they were part of the new civilization.

The multinational crew, however, he had gotten to know over the course of ten days.

He learned that he was on the fence whether he liked Commander Merks. He respected him, wasn't crazy about him. It wasn't that he was mean, he just wasn't very nice, plus he was pretty hardcore and a stickler about rules that actually didn't apply to the Robinson Mission.

Merks was from Germany but spoke flawless English. According to Sam, he spoke flawless Japanese as well, plus about six other languages.

He was tall guy like Tucker, but much fitter. He had dark hair that he kept super short, and he'd even asked Tucker if he planned to get a haircut. Tucker didn't see the point. Somehow when he heard the commander was German he expected a blonde-haired man. The blonde guy was Goncherov or, as he liked to be called, Gonk. He was the bridge guy, the cargo guy, and computer guy. He wasn't tall or any other pictorial Tucker had in his mind about Russians. He was average and smiled a lot. Tucker just wished he understood him better so he could really laugh at the jokes instead of pretending.

The ship's doctor was Len Andros. Tucker had spent the least amount of time with him, and with Jenny, or rather Jennifer Pusk, who was an engineer.

Sam, of course, Tucker was getting to know well, and he was glad Sam was the co-pilot. He didn't know Merks's experience with flying, but he trusted Sam.

Everyone was already onboard and Tucker wanted to eye the civilians. To get a feel for how they were acting and if they were scared.

Out of seventeen civilians, there were ten adults, two teenagers, and five small children. Tucker wasn't good on guessing ages, he just categorized them as 'under his hip in height' young.

"Tucker," Marshman called to him. "Glad I caught you before I went to control and you to the ship. I was just there wishing everyone good luck."

"I wasn't there."

"I see that." Marshman handed him a small drive.

"What's this?"

"You asked for it. I got it. I didn't think I would be able to," Marshman said. "Just plug it into the system and it will play on the monitor in the civilian cabin."

"Oh, that is fantastic." Tucker hadn't told anyone about it and even forgot himself about the movie he needed Marshman to get. "Thank you so much. This is great! I brought some others and loaded them on a drive just in case you couldn't find it. I didn't expect you to. I take this as a good sign."

"I don't know why." Marshman shook Tucker's hand and gave a firm squeeze of support to his arm. "Good luck."

"Thank you, sir," Tucker said. He slipped the drive into his pocket then he turned to look at the families again.

There was a little girl there, her finger in her mouth. Her dark blonde hair hung partly over her face. She looked scared and held the hand of a little boy.

Tucker was going to go to the ship, but instead he walked up to the family, nodded to who he believed was the mother, then crouched down to the level of the little girl.

"Hey," Tucker said. "You scared?"

She nodded.

"Well, don't be. It's gonna be just fine. My buddy, Sam, is flying the plane and, well, he's the best. Okay."

Again, she nodded.

"Is this your brother?" he asked.

"Yes," she replied meekly.

"Brothers are a good thing. Big sisters are the best, you watch out for him always." He stood, then rubbed her head and again nodded acknowledgement to the parents as he made his way to the ship.

"About time," Sam said the second Tucker stepped on board. "Thought you somehow snuck off with Quinn."

"Wouldn't he have liked that," Tucker joked. "Everyone else is ready?"

"Yep."

"Okay, I'm gonna go back to the cargo and wait until they close."

"Gonk is already there," Sam said.

"Never hurts to double-check. Gosh, I hope he doesn't tell any jokes."

"Why?" Sam asked. "He's so funny."

"I don't understand him."

"Well, just laugh because he's funny."

"That's what I do." Tucker took a step and stopped. "Oh, hey, look what I got." He reached into his pocket and lifted the drive.

"What is it?"

"It's the in-flight movie for the civilians."

"The one we already have?" Sam asked.

"No, different."

"You know, they hired a really good production company to make the videos for living on a new planet," Sam said. "They're good."

"Yeah, they are, and made by the same people who did all those Omni-4 videos. I can tell they used the same aliens. But this one, it's even more educational and entertaining."

"It is?"

"It really is," Tucker stated.

"Wow, that's great. They can watch the other ones at a later time. What...what is it called?" Sam asked.

Tucker grinned. "You'll have to wait to find out."

"Do I...want to know?"

Tucker's response was a grin. He playfully tossed up the drive, caught it, put it back in his pocket, and walked off.

They punched through the atmosphere smoothly, but that didn't surprise Tucker. The moment Merks announced that everyone could remove their helmets until Androski entry, there were cheers that carried from the civilian cabin.

Once he was more comfortable with his helmet off, Tucker undid his belt.

"Headed somewhere?" Sam asked.

"Was gonna start the film," Tucker said. "It's all ready to go."

"If it's all in place," Sam said, "I can start it from here. You don't need to go back."

"Really? Sweet," Tucker said. "The floating stuff makes my stomach flip." He inched his way back into the seat.

Sam laughed. "We still have to float, we have systems checks to do."

"Dang it."

"I'm curious, though, what the video is," Sam said.

"You'll find out. Commander Merks, may I announce?"

"Sure." He handed the microphone to Tucker.

Tucker gripped it in his hand. "Ladies and gentlemen, we have now breached the atmosphere and are sailing nicely through space. If you look to your right, you can catch a glimpse of mars. This is a short flight, no snacks will be served. However, for your entertainment and education we have begun your in-flight movie. We hope you find it beneficial about space and life on another planet. Thank you."

Sam reached over and started it. "Okay, it's playing. Now, what is it?"

Tucker smiled. *"Planet of the Apes."*

TEN

A hush took over the ship. A silence so thick it couldn't be penetrated.

It was the moment.

They knew that they would lose power the moment they slipped through the Androski. Everything would power down, and there'd be no life support.

Once they passed through, Merks and Sam had to be fast. They only had a matter of seconds to power back up and gain control of the ship before the gravity of Planet X pulled at them.

Not that they couldn't get out, they could, but it would use all their power.

It was a chance they could not take; they needed that power to circle the planet to find a place to land.

Everyone had suited back up, helmets on.

It was time.

"Prepare for shutdown," Merks said through the crew-only radio system.

"Preparing for shutdown," Sam repeated.

"On my call once we get through, fire up the engines. I'll steer us from the pull."

"Roger that," Sam replied.

"Officer Pusk, I need a systems check as soon as we are through. Check for damage."

"Yes, sir," she replied.

"Freeman and Doc, you'll head to the back to check on our civilians. Keep them focused. Make sure they're alright."

Tucker replied his agreement to the order.

"Here we go," Merks announced.

The Androski was fully visible and there was no doubt when they went through.

Every electronics system on the ship shut down as streaming lights flashed around them outside.

The ship turned slightly sideways and for fourteen seconds they were floating, out of control.

It was the longest fourteen seconds Tucker ever experienced. His heart raced out of control, he could hear his own breathing. He tried to keep that steady.

Even though Tucker was prepared he wasn't ready to find themselves facing the big blue planet. It was all encompassing and blocked everything from view.

As they emerged on the other side, Sam was ready. He powered the ship, the lights came on quickly and the controls returned.

"Shit," Merks said in a calm voice and steered the ship. They tilted even more to the side, and for a moment Tucker thought they were going to hit the planet or get pulled into its gravity.

Merks relied on Sam's help, and while it seemed like they just skimmed by and missed the planet, Tucker was sure they were farther away than it looked.

"Clear," Merks said. "That was close."

"Let's you know how good Omni's pilots had to be," Sam replied.

"Unless they didn't make it," Merks said. "They weren't wearing their helmets when they went through, we know that from transmissions. Fourteen seconds without oxygen.

What are the odds they woke up in enough time to do what we just did?"

"It never dawned on me," Sam said. "I didn't think it would be this fast. I didn't think the planet would be right there. It didn't look it from the probe."

"Now we know," Merks said. "At least everyone coming through after us is informed." He raised his hands to the control. "Alright everyone, you can take off the suits and do the checks."

Tucker kept his mind on Omni-4.

He hadn't really thought too much or for too long before that moment about them going through the Androski and what happened when they emerged.

To Tucker they went right to the planet, all well and fine. Just like they were now.

He'd lived and breathed all knowledge about that mission. Followed all the fictional episodes that some production company created and aired. Tucker had watched them so many times they actually seemed real to him. It was a scary prospect and he could only imagine the terror the crew of Omni-4 must have felt. Unlike the Robinson Mission they had no idea they would lose power. They went in blind, passed out. Waking up to see that planet.

Waking up to see just how close, how tight the pull was and how there was very little time to pull out.

All those years, Tucker believed them to be alive. All those years he waited for the day when he would meet them on the Noah.

Unfortunately, Tucker was facing the reality here: Omni-4 had crashed into Planet X, and the chance to meet them...would never come.

ELEVEN

Three of the crew, Merks, Gonk, and Jenny, hovered behind Sam as he pulled up images of the surface below. They came in fast and all Sam could do was organize them in a grid.

Jenny asked, "What are we looking at exactly?"

"Eastern hemisphere," Sam replied. "That's what's below."

"They're so dark," Jenny said.

"It's night."

"No kidding." Jenny lightly backhanded his shoulder.

"We should be back around to the western hemisphere in about fifteen minutes," Merks said. "We need to figure out where we are landing."

"We need Tuck, he's about the closest we have to a geologist," Sam said.

"I heard my name," Tucker said upon his entrance into the cabin. "What's going on?"

"We're looking at images coming in from down below," Sam said. "We hope you know what you're looking at."

"Nope, haven't a clue." Tucker paused. "Just kidding, of course I do. Don't you?"

"Not really," Sam replied. "None of us do."

"How are things in the back?" Merks asked.

"Some air sickness, some nerves. Doc is handling things. Man, can you imagine how they'll be when they find out we're actually on Earth again."

"That kind of shock," Merks said, "is what we're trying to avoid. No Statue of Liberty moments for these people. We need to break it to them easy. And we're looking for a place to land."

Jenny spoke up. "If I didn't know better, I'd swear we went back millions of years."

"What makes you know better?" Tucker asked. "Did you see something?"

"Actually…pull up that image again," Merks instructed Sam.

Sam did. "Looks like a community. Village or something. It's pretty large, I mean, it's not small."

"Can it be that we arrived after the ARC?" Tucker asked. "And that's one of their communities."

"It's possible," Sam replied.

Gonk pointed to the screen and another image. "This here was Russia, no?"

Tucker just stared at him.

Sam clarified. "It's the eastern hemisphere, yes."

"Then it is, what they call…" Gonk said. "Pangea?"

"Huh?" Tucker questioned, then got it. "Oh! No. No no."

"What do you mean, no?" Sam asked. "It's all one big body of land and a few islands big and small."

"No, it's not," Tucker replied. "Don't confuse millions of years of evolution with a change in oceans. Not saying it won't be, but right now it's not. When the big blue ball started making its way to us, that caused the disasters. Once it settled into orbit, it settled. It made some changes. The oceans are it. Look how nasty the Atlantic is." Tucker whistled. "Not sure the Sharm could handle that. You have the moon

67

pulling one side of the earth, the big blue ball pulling on the other...high tide is pretty interesting, I bet. All this"—he ran his hand down the edge of an image—"is beach that probably goes away at high tide, at least for a couple hours."

Sam laughed. "No way, that's gotta be a hundred miles."

"Probably more. I told you the oceans are a mess," Tucker stated.

"I'm sorry," Sam said. "You're the big farming guy, but this looks like a lot of the continents came together."

Tucker tilted his head. "No. Well...okay, I can see how you can see that. I just wished this computer had one of those photoshop programs where we can pull up an outline of the United States and put it over this."

"I can pull up an overlay." Sam clicked on the keyboard and an outline of the states appeared.

"Now...just...move..." Tucker reached forward and placed his finger on the screen."

"It's not a touch screen," Sam said.

"What?" Tucker laughed. "All this technology and you don't have a touch screen. Man, is this that 1993 stuff you took from JAXA?"

"Ha-ha. Where do you want it?"

"Over...this." Tucker pointed to the land mass. "Down a little, a little more, to the left, a bit more...Bingo."

"Whoa." Sam sat back.

"I see it," Merks said.

"The oceans really shifted?" Jenny asked.

"They did. High tide brings some back, not all. For example, I'm guessing this is Jersey. Look how far inland it appears. By looking at this, the tide comes within fifty miles, but a bit north, well, it slams. Got an ocean shelf that is smooth so that tells me it goes under water a lot. On the other side of the country..." Tucker moved his finger.

"Southern California is gone, so are parts of Mexico. Florida looks like it's back. Most interesting is up here. Can you shift to Alaska?" he asked Sam. "Northern Canada?"

Sam did as requested.

"Look how green it is," Tucker said. "Not a frozen tundra anymore, and in case you're wondering, Alaska didn't grow. That right there used to be the Bering Strait. Water doesn't touch that. It's connected now, and extends far into what we know as Russia. So, look, Gonk." Tucker tapped him on the shoulder. "You can walk home."

"Speaking of home," Merks said. "We need to land and soon. I don't want to land too far from that village, but I don't want to land too close to where these people will get their George Taylor moment."

"Ha!" Tucker blurted a laugh. "Look at you, Commander, knowing the name of the *Planet of the Apes* main character."

"Some of us do know that movie," Merks said. "So here is where the village is. Any suggestions on where we can put this ship down. I want to send teams out. Leave two people behind."

Sam asked, "Maybe a team could head toward the village?"

Merks nodded. "Maybe."

Tucker tapped his finger on his lip. "Sam, I hate to be a pest, but can you enlarge the area around the village, please?" He examined it when the area was enlarged for his benefit.

"Anything?" Merks asked.

"Yep. Found it. Right here." Tucker pointed. "That looks like a good area. Far enough inland to be away from the tides. I'm not seeing any fissures from massive quakes, like I saw further north. Yeah, there."

Merks turned to Sam. "Plug in those coordinates. Tucker, will you go prepare the civilian cabin for landing."

"Absolutely." He turned and exited the cabin.

Sam's hand moved as he punched in numbers.

"I hope he's right," Merks said.

"I'm sure he is," Sam replied.

"Doesn't matter now, I guess," Merks said. "We're locked in. We're landing." He looked to the faces of the crew still around him. "Welcome home...again."

Tucker peered up to the sky, shading his eyes, before making a notation on a clipboard. They had been on the ground for about ninety minutes. Following the enthusiasm and fear from the civilians, Merks had instructed them they could disembark but they were not to go far until the teams returned.

Tucker knew the translation of that. Merks wanted to check out the village, make sure it was safe and then figure out how to get everyone there.

A safe perimeter was set up around the ship, and orange sticks that looked like the ones Tucker used to put out on the farm marked where they would mow. Only they weren't just marking sticks, they had beams on them to sound an alarm should any animals or danger cross.

Gonk set them up with Merks.

Sam and Jenny were busy helping to get stuff ready for the scouting trips. They unloaded the solar buggies and put the finishing touches on them, while Tucker did his own thing.

He was excited to get out there. He knew what he saw on the image, or what he thought he saw, and it was a good destination to search out.

It would give him a glimpse into the final happenings on Earth, at least a little, and judging by the structural remains he saw on the scan, it wasn't hit too badly. Tucker was curious as to why that was.

Commander Merks and Pusk would be the ones to venture to the village. If it were a viable place to go and, of course, if they were invited to join the village, they would start moving the civilians. Tucker was still on the fence about joining an already established community, even temporarily. The reason for the relocation of the four rich families from an earth in danger was to colonize. To start anew and live.

Sure it would be simple to just toss them into an established community, but something inside of Tucker longed to branch out. Not toss all the eggs—or people—into one basket.

He and Sam planned a slightly longer journey with that in mind. Not only to see the ruins of the city but take a few days to see what was around. What was viable. Where they could start their own community near the village.

After looking at the sky one more time, he tucked his clipboard under his arm and fixed his watch.

"Really?" Merks walked up behind him. "You adjusted the time."

"Yes, sir, I did. Unless the sun changed I am gonna guess it's about ten fifteen in the morning."

"Good to know."

"Did you see how pretty the big blue is in the sky? It's like when you used to see the moon during the day."

"Looks pretty incredible, like we are on some other planet."

"Anyone making any guesses?" Tucker asked. "I mean, after seeing the movie that had to cross their minds."

"You know more than me, I saw you talking to them."

"That's because I needed to know if anyone had some know-how. We're leaving Gonk and he's not very trained."

"In?"

"Well, knowing the volatile history of this planet. I set up a seismograph and a barometer to monitor activity. We need someone to watch to see if we are getting increases or changes quickly coming in the weather."

Merks nodded, impressed. "Very good thinking. Did you find anyone?"

"As a matter of fact, surprisingly one of the families has a daughter that wanted to be a weather girl," Tucker said. "I know what you're thinking, 'oh boy, a weather girl, probably flighty and did it for the fame.'"

"Actually, that wasn't what I was thinking."

"Oh, okay," Tucker said. "Maybe it was just me. But they actually have to learn the stuff. Had to give her some quick tips on the seismic activity but she seems pretty quick and smart. I gave her a tablet; she'll watch the readings and let Gonk know if there's a problem."

"Do you think maybe I should stay behind in case I should move the ship?" Merks asked. "What are your readings now?"

"Good. I mean. I think we're fine. I really do," Tucker said. "Should take you a couple hours to get to the village. Jenny can handle any problems you two encounter on the road. Sam's GPS system should lead you there with minimal problems. I think the only worry you should have is problems with the natives."

"True.

"Maybe bring a gift," Tucker suggested. "They've probably been there a while. We don't even know if they're part of the ARC."

"They could be descendants of survivors. Let me think on the gift. And, Tucker, it's good to have you on the team."

"Well, that's nice of you to say now that we're here." Tucker smiled. "I wouldn't have it any other way." He looked over his shoulder. "I see Sam is ready. I wanna give this clipboard to Matty," he said. "I want her to chart her readings."

"Sounds good." He extended his hand. "Good luck, and though we don't know if it's possible, make sure you at least try to stay in contact."

"Will do." Tucker shook his hand and, with that clipboard, sought out Matty to discuss readings one more time.

Tucker was excited to get going. He wanted to see what was out there. They may have known where they were, but the 'when' was still up in the air. Tucker knew, just by the ruins that remained, they were nowhere near as far in the future as the landscape suggested.

Hopefully with the exploration they'd get a good idea of how far into the future they'd jumped.

TWELVE

A strange, steady breeze made controlling the buggy diffi-cult at times. It was odd to Merks, relying on a GPS that didn't mention roads. Only an electronic sounding voice stat-ing commands like 'stay left' and 'in one hundred feet clear-ing moves to the right.'

It was a good thing the system had imaging, which Pusk watched as Merks drove.

At least six times they had to stop on the fifty-three-mile journey to look for themselves because it looked like they were driving right into a wall.

"They travel outside their village," Pusk said. "Carriages, horses…they've been this way."

"There are clearings."

She nodded. "Which leaves me to wonder if they are the only village, or if there are others."

"We didn't spot any."

"Doesn't mean that they aren't there," she said. "Stop."

"Why?" Merks asked as he brought the buggy to a halt. "Are we there?"

"Not quite. Almost. But we can't go any further," she said. "There's a wall."

"I don't see it. Just trees."

"Another fifty feet it will come into view."

"Does the system say it's a wall?"

Pusk held up the small tablet. The images weren't satellite images. They were real-time diagrams collected by the scanner on the buggy. Blue background with light blue 3D style line drawings.

Merks continued driving, this time slower. The GPS didn't call out any commands, there really wasn't anywhere to go. It looked like a forest before them.

He pulled over then took a minute to disconnect the starter for safe keeping. He grabbed a backpack, Pusk grabbed hers, and they headed to the woods.

"The wall is right ahead. I don't know how we're missing it," she said. "Scan says it's twenty feet high."

"The trees are thick. Are we headed in the right direction at least?"

"We are. The village is a half-mile from where we are. Not far from the wall."

"If they built a twenty-foot wall, makes me wonder what they're trying to keep out."

A snap of a twig drew Merks's attention, and he extended his arm, stopping Pusk. "Did you hear that?" he asked.

"I didn't. Maybe it's an animal."

Another snaping sound and within seconds, the crunch of footsteps carried their way.

Before they could react or even comprehend what was happening, four men appeared before them. One carried a rifle, the other three bows and arrows.

"Stop right there," the man with the rifle said. He was a younger man, early twenties.

Merk raised his hands. "We mean no harm."

"I know that," he said.

One of the men called out, "Is that more of them, Pyle?"

"Looks that way," Pyle replied. "Just not sure which ones." He lowered the rifle. "You can put down your hands.

I see the uniform. Though I'm not familiar with IRM." Pyle referenced the patch on Merks's jumpsuit uniform. "Merks? Does it say?"

"Merks is my last name. Commander Robert Merks," he answered. "IRM stands for International Robinson Mission."

"Not familiar with that either, maybe our leader is. This way." Pyle signaled his men to go forward while he stayed close to Merks and Pusk, leading them through the woods.

It wasn't long before they reached the wall that Pusk had mentioned. It was constructed out of trees, and when Merks saw it he looked up. "This is taller than twenty feet."

"Makes you think of *King Kong*," she replied in a whisper.

"I didn't want to be the one to say it."

Pyle whistled loud and short, and a portion of the wall slid open like a gate.

There were several people just inside who watched them walk in. Merks could see the village in the distance, smoke from chimneys rising up.

As they walked a bit further a man hurried to them. He looked to be in his sixties and in good shape. He carried something in his hand and Merks could see that the man smiled.

But as soon as the man was close enough, the smile dropped from his face and was replaced with a look of disappointment.

"This is our leader," Pyle said.

"Why do you introduce me like that," the man said. "I'm sorry. I…saw the craft fly over and the blue streak, I thought for sure…I thought for sure you were someone I knew. I even brought him something."

"Who…who did you think we were?" Merks asked.

"The Robinson."

"We are," Merks replied.

"Well...is Tucker Freeman alright?"

Pusk let out a short laugh. "He's fine. You know Tucker? Sorry, I know that's not funny, but a desolate, changed Earth, God knows how far in the future..."

"For you guys, a hundred and forty-two years," he said.

"Christ," Merks gasped.

Pusk found it even more amusing. "Over a hundred years into the future and one of the first people we meet knows Tucker? How is that possible?"

"Long story," the man answered. "I was convinced he was here. I even"—he held up the container—"brought him milk. It's a...it's an inside joke."

"You can put that away for now," Merks said, "and give it to him later. He's on another scouting team."

"I will. And I'm sorry, I didn't introduce myself." He held out his hand. "Joshua. Joshua Quinn. We left Earth the same time as you. I'm the commander of the Genesis project."

"Did I ever tell you," Sam spoke slightly out of breath as he and Tucker walked, "I'm not a physical person?" Walking was understating. Since leaving the buggy, they climbed over things, through things, and once under.

"This isn't physical," Tucker said with a chuckle.

"You don't think?"

"We've only been walking twenty minutes. You're funny."

"I'm serious. It's been years since I did anything physical. I'm a desk guy. I use a JAXA discontinued Robot Max to get my beverages from the fridge at home and sweep my floors."

"So funny, I'm surprised you didn't pack him."

Sam stopped walking.

"You did?" Tucker laughed even harder. "You packed your housekeeper."

"It was a pretty brilliant invention," Sam said. "Four feet tall, light weight. Just because it tried to kill someone once...once, they scrapped it."

"That's a shame."

"Okay, you know what? I have to stop." Sam bent over slightly grabbing his knees.

"We're almost there. I know we're close. In fact, you'll get a kick out of this."

"I doubt it."

"You and I, we're about ten feet from a road. Well, what's left of one. Bet it'll be easier to walk."

"We've been walking on the side of a road?"

"Yeah."

"I hate you," Sam said. "How do you know?"

"Well, aside from the fact I can see it sort of, this..." Tucker stomped his foot causing a 'thunk' sound.

"What the hell was that?"

"A sign. Not like...oh, a heavenly sign, but a sign. Look." Tucker pointed down.

How he even saw it, Sam didn't know. It was completely buried, all but a tiny bit of a rusted corner emerging from the ground, along with part of the metal post. Erosion or a storm had probably brought it to the surface.

"This way." Tucker led the way up the small grade. "No more physical walking. Well, one more time. I think this used to be a guardrail." He felt through the brush. "Yes, it is. But let me clear it for you."

Tucker pulled branches and weeds creating a small enough opening for Sam to climb over.

On the other side of the rail, Tucker waited for Sam.

Sam stumbled a bit as he climbed from the other side of the guardrail. "Why do you look so tall?" Sam asked.

"That's because I am."

"You're not that tall." Sam held out his hand for Tucker to help him over. As soon as he cleared the rail, he realized why Tucker looked so tall. The road on the other side had grown over or lifted so much it was nearly even with the rail.

"Man, you really aren't physical," Tucker said.

"I'm tired from walking and climbing. I think I need an energy bar or something."

"They don't really give you energy. We can stop if you want. I think it's a straight shot now to where we're heading."

Sam stood there looking around. If it was a highway, it was lumpy. But they weren't lumps or mounds, they were cars. Nature had encompassed and devoured them until they became part of the landscape. "Cars. We're walking on cars."

"Looks like an exodus," Tucker replied. "Did you want to stop, you didn't say."

"How far do you think we are?" Sam asked.

Tucker pointed outward. "See for yourself."

Sam looked. "Holy shit. Holy…fucking shit."

"That's your *Planet of the Apes* moment, isn't it?" Tucker asked.

"Yeah, yeah it is," Sam replied. "Is that yours, too?"

"Nah, but I'll let you know when I see it."

"I think I need to pause." Sam set down his bag. He sat down on one of the mounds.

He needed more than just to take a break. It wasn't that their destination was all that far ahead. They were actually close. Sam needed to take minute to absorb when he saw his *Planet of the Apes* moment. It was worn some, perhaps overgrown, but from the distance Sam couldn't see any damage. It was the defining moment that reiterated what had happened to the world and that they truly were in the future. It was hard to believe it was still there, still standing and he couldn't take his eyes off of the Washington Monument that poked high above the wilderness and trees ahead of them.

PART THREE: MERGER

THIRTEEN

Nate Gale traced his finger over the rounded edge of the shoe imprint in the dirt. "They don't care that they're leaving a trail." He brushed his hands off as he stood. "They're still together. Two of them. They're walking."

Curt shook his head. "Tell me again why we're following them?"

"Well, Clutch," Nate sarcastically called him by his nickname. "We need to know if they are from the ARC...or somewhere else."

"Why?"

Finch grumbled. "Does it matter? We should look for them. But..." He faced his crew. "I think Ben should stay back. He's barely walking as it is from his injuries."

"Yes," Ben said. "Everyone keeps forgetting since landing in this godforsaken version of Earth, I have been the Kenny from *South Park*. If you don't get that reference"—he looked at Rey—"I don't know what to tell you."

"Me?" Rey laughed. "I get the reference."

"I don't," Nate said.

"Me either," said Westerman. Of course he wouldn't know, he was born in the future far after even an inkling of the laugh out loud television show remained.

"*South Park* was a cartoon," Rey explained. "The Kenny character died or was hurt in every episode."

Westerman laughed. "Really?"

Rey nodded. "Yep."

"What's a cartoon?" Westerman asked.

"I'll stay with him." Sandra lifted her hand. "He and I will walk back to the ship. Make sure your tracking is on. We'll be in close enough range to pick you up, and if there are any problems we can come and get you."

"I'll stay with them, too," Westerman stated. "In case anything strange happens."

"Like what?" Finch asked.

Westerman shrugged. "I don't know. Strange. Like an animal I know but you don't."

"Great." Ben tossed out his hand. "You know if one of us gets attacked by a mutant future animal, it's going to be me."

"Probably," Finch said. "But you have Westerman. You're good. Let's put a time limit down. If we don't find these people, we head back."

"Three hours?" Sandra suggested.

It was a plan, but before they continued on following the footsteps, Finch had Curt and Nate stay with the footprints while he and Rey went back to the ship with the others.

Finch wanted to get flag markers. A lot of landmarks and areas were overgrown and he didn't want them to lose their way back.

"What?" Nate asked Curt. "You're just staring at me."

"I'm not staring at you, I'm thinking. I mean, who could they be? Could they be natives?"

"We have their solar charger."

"But think about it," Curt said. "Who's to say they didn't take it from Quinn's people or the group that fractioned off from Quinn."

"I didn't think of that."

"So, should we really go find them?"

"Yes," Nate replied. "Anyone we talk to is a source of information for us. We're stuck here for the rest of our lives and I for one would like to know what we're in for."

"What kind of future animals do you think they have?"

"I don't know. I'm a geologist not zoologist."

"I'm just making idle conversation. Which way did you vote to go?" Curt asked.

"Excuse me?"

"Stay or hit the Androski? Three of us voted to go, three voted to stay. Which way did you vote?"

"They call it a secret vote for a reason," Nate said.

"Oh, stop, which way did you vote? I voted to stay." Curt shrugged. "Why bother trying to go back or to a future that could be worse?"

"Because no matter where we go, there's nothing there for us," Nate replied.

"So you decided to take a spin on the wheel of future."

"I did."

"Crazy." Curt shook his head. "I wonder who the other two were."

"Us." Finch's voice carried to them from behind as he and Rey returned. "We did."

"Why?" Curt asked.

Rey answered, "Me, I was kind of hoping we'd hit the time-travel jackpot and end up with the dinosaurs."

"Great…" Curt growled out the word. "And you know, Ben being there means we'd arrive when the extinction meteor hit."

Finch shook his head. "Let's just follow the footprints."

Nate led the way. "They definitely are walking together. It looks like they keep stopping though. One set stops. Like here." He pointed. "The other kind of moves around in small circles."

"Like he's antsy?" Rey asked.

"Yes. Maybe the one is hurt," Nate suggested.

"Or old," Curt said. "They can't keep up."

"Then why are they walking here?" Finch asked. "They set up a campsite, so obviously they don't belong."

"Maybe it's a local tourist attraction," Rey said. "I know that sounds silly, but maybe they're both young and it's like a thing for young people to sneak off to the forbidden or verboten zone."

"That's a good point," Finch said.

"I did that as a kid," Curt said. "We all did. By chance did Quinn mention if any of the ancestor cities were this way, I mean the original cities built after the event?"

Finch shook his head. "I think he said they're out west, but maybe he doesn't know about one this way."

"I know we found the solar charger," Curt said. "But like I was telling Nate, we don't know if whoever had it stole it or found it. They have to be natives or part of the other Genesis group. The ARC hasn't shown up according to Quinn so who else would have flown through?"

"That..." Finch pointed. "Is a good point. Maybe the ARC did show up."

"I find it hard to believe," Rey stated. "Quinn didn't see them. He watches the skies."

"It's a big sky," Finch replied.

"Whoever they are...they're definitely headed somewhere." Nate followed the trail, walking a little ahead of everyone else. "They know where they're going."

"I was thinking," Rey said, "you know what's funny."

"Funny?" Finch asked. "You're finding something funny? I would love to hear what you're finding funny."

"Maybe not funny, but ironic," Rey said. "Quinn told us Wyoming was a safe state. Nothing ever happened there, right?"

"Right."

"That means Yellowstone never erupted. All those years they kept saying it would blow," Rey said. "And the world shook and shifted and it still didn't go off."

"That is funny in an ironic way," Finch said, then noticed Nate had stopped. "Nate, what's wrong?"

"They stopped. I mean." Nate turned around. "When I crossed that patch of weeds, they just disappeared."

"Maybe they veered off before that," Curt suggested. "Everyone look around."

"Oh, there," Rey said. "Right there before the weeds."

Curt laughed. "The mighty tracker missed it."

"I'm not a tracker." Nate started walking back. "I'm a..." His startled scream faded with an echo as he suddenly dropped out of sight.

"Nate!" Finch shouted, charging forth.

"Stay back!" Curt held out his hand. "We have to be careful." He inched forward. "Nate!"

A distant groan carried to them. "I'm okay," Nate replied, his voice sounding deep and hollow. "The thingy broke my fall. I'm fine. I think."

"The thingy?" Curt looked questioningly at Finch. He then inched a little more. As soon as he neared the weed patch that Nate was talking about he saw the opening in the ground. "I found him."

"Nate!" Finch called. "I have a rope, we'll pull you up. How unstable do you think this area is?"

"I don't think it's unstable, just...where someone tried to block off a stairwell," Nate called up. "Guys? I think you should come down here. You should see this."

The bouncing sound to Nate's voice really made Finch curious. He and Rey joined Curt.

Curt stood at the edge of the opening, staring down. A slate of concrete had fallen into the opening. It had collapsed in a slanted way, acting like a steep slide, the edge of which rested on the first landing of a long staircase. He glanced over his shoulder to Finch. "It's the old Metro."

◇◇◇◇

Curt secured a line onto the remnants of an old railing. It felt strong enough, and he tested it first, climbing down on the slanted slab of concrete. He waited on the first landing for Rey. She descended next, followed by Finch.

All three of them turned on their flashlights, which gave them plenty of light to make it down the stairs.

Nate's beam of light moved back and forth. He was at the bottom of the staircase.

"You alright?" Finch asked. "You're not injured?"

"I probably would have been if I'd rolled down the stairs," Nate said. "Fortunately, I'm not Ben."

"Hey, Curt," Rey said. "You think because he wasn't falling to his death was the reason you failed to...clutch him?"

"Yeah," Nate said. "Why didn't you clutch me?"

"First of all, that's not funny. Second...he was fifteen feet away," Curt defended.

"Why exactly are we down here?" Finch asked.

"This is amazing," Nate stated. "It stayed structurally strong."

"That we know of," Finch said.

"But that's not it. Look what I found as soon as I came down the stairs," Nate said.

"Why did you go down the steps?" Finch asked. "That was dangerous."

"I know, but I saw it..." Nate pointed to flat metal object near the edge of the wall at the bottom of the stairs. "I think the reason that blockade collapsed is because they poked a hole in it. It weakened it."

"Who?" Finch asked.

"Whoever lived here," Nate replied. "This is a stove. Well, they used it as a stove. A big one too. Smoke would carry up the staircase. This whole area..." Nate walked a few feet. "Look at the tables. They moved them down here. Like this was the main cafeteria."

Curt walked to a table. "There are ten tables. That's a lot of people."

Rey ran her hand over one of the tables. "It's dusty but not ruined by mold or humidity."

"So a civilization was here for a while," Finch said. "How long ago?"

"Maybe fifty years by the coloring," Nate said. "Still, this part of the county with all that happened? Did they move here or hunker down here? That's what I want to know."

"It's not important," Curt said. "Is it?"

Before Nate could answer, a male sounding shriek of surprise echoed to them. It was as if someone in the distance of the subway saw something that startled him.

Rey jumped. "Someone's here."

Finch pulled out his pistol and spun to the sound. When he did, he was blasted by two bright lights. He tried to shield his eyes, keeping his aim steady.

"It is him!" the male voice shouted.

"There is no way," another male said.

"I'm telling you. I'd recognize that face anywhere. It's Commander Finch. Holy shit, it's The Clutch. It's the crew of the Omni-4. Some of them."

One light went down to the ground as the other man said, "Well, let's not blind them."

Finch still held aim, even though he was bewildered.

Rey looked at Finch. "We are so popular in the apocalypse."

The two men emerged from the shadows, their lights lowered. They weren't flashlights like Finch and the others carried, or even spotlights. They were rectangular and exceptionally bright.

"I knew it," the taller man with the country accent said, rambling excitedly. "I knew you guys were alive. I just knew it. Didn't I think that, Sam? Maybe I didn't say it after Merks was all like, 'no way could their commander snap to consciousness and not hit the big blue.' That's what he said. Did you guys fall down that hole? There's an easier way down here, you know. Oh, gees, where are my manners. By the way"—he extended his hand to Finch—"I'm Tucker Freeman."

FOURTEEN

The new guy, Tucker, just liked to talk. He carried on a conversation about some guy named Merks and how cool the White House was, but he didn't give any real information. Finch barely understood. He did lead them all the way to the open staircase of the subway and Finch figured he'd wait until they were outside and no longer trapped to get a grasp on what he was talking about. He knew by the way he spoke he wasn't a native, and by the way they dressed in their uniform jumpsuits similar to the Omni's they weren't part of Genesis. "Okay, please, stop. I would love to hear more but…How do you two know us?"

"Him," Sam said. "Not me. I've heard of you. This guy has followed your story since he was a kid."

"Oh boy," Rey said. "How long after us did you leave?"

"Twenty-five years," Sam replied.

"Twenty-five years?" Nate asked. "Same time as Genesis."

"Three weeks before," Sam answered. "We were part of a private civilian funded mission. Partially civilian funded."

"I wanted to be on the Genesis," Tucker said. "But I wasn't picked."

"He should have been," Sam replied. "The contributions he's made to man's long-term survival are insane. But he's with us."

91

"Yeah, good thing," Nate stated. "You'd be around sixty now."

Finch explained, "Genesis landed here twenty-seven years ago."

"Have you seen them?" Sam asked. "Quinn?"

Finch nodded. "We have. They're well."

"For us it was like last week that we saw them," Tucker said.

"Then they'll look older to you," Finch said. "But I bet they'll be glad to know you're alive."

"They probably know by now," Tucker replied. "Yesterday we split off in teams to scout. Our commander set out for a village near where Baltimore would be. Was that them?"

Rey replied, "It is. And this...this is fantastic."

"What are you guys doing in D.C.?" Tucker asked. "Did you land here?"

"No," Curt said. "We landed in a pretty bad area. Worst place imaginable. Worst place we could have landed. But, hey, we're still learning. We haven't been here that long. We're more sightseeing the revamped Earth."

"I'm surprised you didn't see our ship," Nate said. "In the Potomac?"

"You landed the ship in the Potomac?" Tucker asked.

"Former," Nate said, "it's a dry bed now."

"That's like...right over that way," Tucker said. "Holy cow. I need to see the Omni."

And just like that, he took off.

Finch looked at Sam. "Is he always so excitable?"

"No, he's really laid back," Sam replied. "It's you guys. He's wanted to be in space since he watched you prepare for the Omni mission, and since he watched that Omni-4 TV show."

"I'm sorry," Finch said. "The what?"

They set up camp for the night next to the Omni, with plans to all return to Quinn's community the next day. Rey could listen to Tucker talk all night because he was so entertaining. He'd never suffered from the shock of learning he landed on a future Earth because, as he explained, they knew going through that would be the outcome.

She was sure he'd wear thin on her but for the time being, as they all sat around the fire, he made them laugh.

"So I cured the alien plague?" Sandra asked.

"It was great and just in time to deliver the alien triplets. That was a surprise," Tucker replied. "I don't know why that wasn't the season finale. Instead, it was Clutch asking Rey to marry him and she said yes."

Rey laughed hard.

Curt looked at her. "That's funny?"

"Yeah, me and you." Rey cleared her throat. "Wouldn't happen. Not that there's anything wrong with you, but *People*'s Sexiest Man alive isn't for me. And I'm never getting attached or in a relationship again. But it's fiction, right?"

Tucker nodded. "That's right. But they had it all wrong from the get-go. There aren't any aliens."

"That we know of," Sam said.

"True. I'm curious," Tucker said. "What was your *Planet of the Apes* moment?"

Rey looked at him curiously. "I'm sorry my what?"

"He has this thing," Sam explained. "Like at the end of *Planet of the Apes* they see the Statue of Liberty and the character of Taylor freaks realizing he's on Earth."

"Uh, Sam," Tucker said, "you needed to say spoiler alert."

"I don't think that matters," Sam said. "Even though we knew, I still had that moment when I saw the Washington Monument."

Rey nodded. "It was the space station. We found a piece of it not far from here. But Finch knew"—she pointed—"before us."

"I found a coin. I just didn't know how to tell them," Finch said.

"What made you guys decide to stay and not hit the Androski again?" Sam asked.

Ben answered, "Some of us did want to and some didn't. We took a vote. Majority would decide, stay or go. Westerman was the deciding factor. Because we split the decision."

"So...why didn't the ones who wanted to go, go?" Sam asked.

Ben shrugged. "It was a matter of leaving the rest behind without the tech, taking the only working ship, because Genesis doesn't work anymore. It didn't matter to me. I wasn't going anywhere."

"Me either," Sandra said. "But I needed the medical tech stuff on board and if they left, I'd lose it."

"Some of us wanted to go," Finch said. "Me, for one. I mean, this really isn't our Earth anymore, so why not see where it takes us next? That was my thought. Who knows, maybe we'd end up able to warn people, tell them the safe places on Earth so people could live."

"Are there any safe places?" Tucker asked.

"Several states went unharmed," Finch said.

"Will you..." Rey stood. "Excuse me for a second. I need to get something to drink." She walked from the circle to the ship, carefully stepping over Westerman who was fast asleep by the door.

As soon as she stepped inside, she heard a loud burst of laughter. Tucker probably said something funny again.

She made her way to the kitchen area, checking cabinets.

"You can't find water or juice?" Finch asked.

His voice startled her and she grasped her chest and spun. "No, I was looking for Curt's stash. I'd like a drink."

Finch reached around her to a drawer and opened it. "One of his hiding spots." He pulled out a bottle and handed it to her.

"Drink?" she asked.

"No, I'm good. Everything okay?"

"Yes." Rey poured a drink into a glass and set the bottle on the counter. "I was thinking about what Ben said."

"About?"

"Why those of us who wanted to leave didn't. It made sense, we couldn't leave Sandy without her med bay."

"Very true," Finch agreed.

"Finch, you heard Sam. The comments he made about the Omni, about how they used to think it was so high-tech and how their ship was far beyond us in technology."

"But they don't have touchscreens," Finch said.

"Yeah, Tucker was shocked about that."

"Why are you thinking about this?" Finch asked.

"If the Lola is far superior than the Omni in all ways, but the touch screen, then...we wouldn't leave Sandra, Ben, and Curt without technology, would we? There would be a viable ship left behind."

"What are you suggesting?"

"I think you know," Rey said. "I think, before it closes, me, you, and whoever else wants to go should hit the Androski. What do you think?"

"I think I need that drink." Finch reached to the cabinet and pulled out a cup. He lifted the bottle and poured some.

"That's not an answer. Seriously," Rey said. "What do you think of my idea?'

"I think...let's do it. Let's go through."

"To the other side?" Rey held up her cup.

Finch tapped his cup to hers. "To the other side."

FIFTEEN

Genesis Village

Silence.

There was complete and utter silence inside the Omni-4 just moments after Finch let the crew know what he and Rey wanted to do.

"As Ben told Tucker and Sam," Finch said, "the reason those of us who wanted to leave didn't was because we couldn't take the ship. The Lola is bigger and has everything you would need. So with a clear conscious, we can do this."

"I don't understand," said Sandra. "There is still so much to see here. How can you make that decision before you have seen everything?"

Nate answered, "Because if they don't go soon, the Androski will close."

"I know you're probably angry," Finch said.

"No." Curt shook his head. "Not angry at all. I understand. I do. This could be one of the last times I see you, Finch."

"I for one," Ben spoke up, "envy his decision. I do. I would go, but I am fearful of going back to a world that is a constant reminder of all that I lost. Here, now, it's not."

"What about you, Nate?" Sandra asked. "What are your thoughts on what they want to do?"

"I think I want to go with them," Nate replied. "Yeah, like Ben, I worry that we may end up right back where we left. But that's a chance I'm willing to take."

Sandra huffed. "Unreal. We all lost. Every one of us lost. But we gained each other. We came through the Androski together. Right here, right now, we know we can survive. It's a gamble, you guys know this, right?"

Finch nodded. "We do. I don't know about all of you, but I was anxious to join this mission to be an explorer, so I want explore. I knew there was a chance we wouldn't go back. And more than likely when we go through the Androski, we won't go back to our time. Maybe we'll get close. Maybe we won't. But we have to see, we have to try, right? As far as I know, no one has ever gone back through."

"The NOAA satellite did," Nate said. "It went through the Androski in 1993 and took pictures pretty much of this planet, right here and now. When it went back through it came in decades later, yes, but close to our time. We may do that as well."

"You all could come with us," Rey said. "You could. We came through as a team, we can leave as a team. Really, what is there for us here?"

Ben stood. "About the same as there is for us back there, less the visual memories everywhere. Look around, Rey. We know what happened to the world. Do you really want to live through it?"

"Let's not do this," Curt said. "We can't guilt them for making a decision and, technically, staying on mission. We were to go through and return. They are. I'm here. I'm not leaving. You guys have your adventure and I'm certain staying here won't be adventure free. Hell, I'm waiting on those future mutant animals to attack Ben."

"Ha, ha, ha." Ben shook his head. "And you know they will."

"When?" Sandra asked. "When will you leave?"

"Since the ship is still packed," Finch said, "and will be fully charged by tomorrow, I say we leave in the afternoon."

"And I say..." Curt stood. "Let's not mope, let's not be angry or sad. Let's get out there and enjoy the welcoming party Quinn threw for the Robinson, and we make the best of this night. I won't say it's a last night. I firmly believe, someway, somehow, in some point in time..." Curt said. "We'll see each other again."

Tiki style torches made up a perimeter around the area that was center of the village.

A single bonfire was in the middle of it all. It was massive and roaring. People laughed and children ran.

Quinn and his people welcomed the newcomers.

Rey walked around a lot, looking at everyone, watching those from the Omni-4 that were staying behind. Perhaps it was a subconscious thing, but Curt, Sandra, and Ben seemed to be going out of their way to be friendly to those who lived in the Genesis Village.

She carried around her cup, and it never seemed to get empty, no matter how many times she took a drink. Someone running around with a jug of wine would pass her and add to her cup.

It was a beautiful cup, hand crafted and ceramic.

She made her way to Tucker who sat with Quinn. They chatted away like two long-lost friends. Even though to Tucker it had only been a week.

"There she is," Quinn said, looking up when Rey approached. "Enjoying your last night in this time?"

"I am. Your community is wonderful," Rey replied. "The Robinson Mission are certainly fortunate to be here."

"Better us than the other half of the Genesis." Quinn held up his cup.

"Whatever happened to them?" Tucker asked. "Did they move far away or did they go back through?"

"If you would have asked me twenty years ago," Quinn said, "I would have told you no, they didn't go back. But the Androski opened back up, and they got ahold of the ship about fifteen years ago."

Rey looked quickly at him. "You said they were dangerous."

"They are and there are plenty of them still around. But there's always a chance some tried to go back," Quinn replied. "We'll never know, will we?"

"No, we won't." Rey caught a glimpse of Finch. He stood off to the side at the edge of the perimeter, staring up to the sky.

After excusing herself, she walked over to him. "Everything okay?"

"Oh, yes, thank you. Just thinking and looking. Tell me…were you always the type at a party that went off by yourself or in a corner to talk to one person?"

"I didn't make it a habit to go to parties outside of my family. But if I did, I preferred smaller groups. You?"

"Yes. I was asking because you and I seem to venture off."

"Are you having second thoughts?" Rey asked.

"Not at all, just looking up. Wondering how many ships have gone through the Androski."

"I don't recall any in our lifetime being lost."

"Just us," Finch said. "Which is a good thing. I mean, anywhere in the future that we go, we won't be like some alien life appearing. We won't be a surprise. They'll know us. Like Tucker, they'll expect one day for a ship to appear. I do."

"Do you believe that?" Rey asked.

"Absolutely I do. As long as we go to the future, they'll know us. Tales from generation to generation."

"Are you scared?" Rey questioned.

"I am nervous. Not about handling this, but nervous about where we will end up," Finch replied.

"Any guesses?"

"Like you, I haven't a clue. But," Finch said, "we will know tomorrow." He looked up again to the sky. "Tomorrow will tell."

SIXTEEN

The last of the fresh supplies were loaded onto the ship. Even though they had food to last a while, Quinn wanted to give them a jump so they could save the long-term surplus.

There was excitement mixed with a certain sadness in the air.

Curt, Sandra, and Ben stood outside the ship, now relocated away from the Genesis village for a better takeoff.

"And this is one of my tablets." Sandra handed it to Nate. "Should you need something, just hit search. The database on this is amazing."

"You don't need it?" Nate asked.

"The Lola has two. I'm good. Make sure you keep a log."

"I will."

She embraced him.

"Well, buddy." Curt held out his hand to Finch. "This is it."

"Not goodbye." Finch shook Curt's hand then brought him in for a quick embrace. "You lead the team. Don't give up on finding what's out there."

"I have no plans to give up. I'll search here, you"—he pointed to the sky—"go there. You're okay with going back through the Androski."

Finch nodded. "I have Nate trained on restarting the engines the second we get through."

"Well, you'll be ready, unlike last time."

"I'll be ready." Finch turned to Ben. "Be careful."

"Is that a comment geared toward the hatred this new Earth has for me?"

"It is. Maybe you should come with us to change your luck."

"No, no." Ben shook his head. "With my luck, I'll lose a limb."

"We better go." Finch turned his head. "Rey, we're ready."

She emerged from the ship, having secured the new supplies. "Did Quinn leave?"

"Didn't you say goodbye?" Finch asked.

"I did, but it was quick." She walked to Curt and hugged him. "Don't settle. Explore this place."

"I got the same advice from Finch," Curt said.

"And Ben." Rey faced him.

"Don't tell me to be careful and don't get hurt," Ben said.

"I was going to tell you to find love."

"Really?"

"No, I was gonna tell you to not get hurt." Rey hugged him. "Thank you for everything. For being the one who believed in me." She kissed him on the cheek. "I'm gonna say bye to Sandra."

Finch nodded and stepped back to the ship's door as Rey walked toward Sandra and Nate. He sucked at goodbyes and just wanted to get going. It wasn't that he didn't want to see his friends for a little more, just that dragging it out made things worse.

As he stepped onto the Omni, Finch heard the beeping of a horn and looked up to see a solar buggy.

It was driven by Commander Merks.

Tucker got out, along with Sam. Finch figured they were saying goodbye, until he saw them lift bags out of the back.

"Glad we caught you," Tucker said. "Let me put these inside and I'll get the rest."

"You're dropping off supplies?" Finch asked.

"Yep, along with me. I kind of figured you could use my help. A full team is always best. I have a tiny bit, tiny bit of medical training. So...here I am."

"You just got here," Finch said. "Your team. Quinn."

"I wanna try to go back, Finch, I do. You'll have me?" Tucker asked.

"Of course."

Sam approached.

"You dropping off or staying?" Finch asked him.

"Last I knew, you didn't have an engineer or a co-pilot," Sam replied, then looked at Curt. "Of course, no one can replace The Clutch."

Curt smiled. "I'm sure you'll be great." He shifted his eyes to Finch. "I feel much better knowing you have a trained co-pilot with you."

Finch leaned into him and whispered, "Me too."

"Hey!" Tucker poked his head out of the door. "I'm thinking since this is a new mission, we should be called Omni-5, what do you think?"

With a tightly closed mouth, Finch shook his head.

"Thought I'd ask." Tucker slipped back into the ship.

"You sure you're ready for that guy?" Curt asked.

"Um..." Finch glanced to the ship. "No."

He laughed about it but the truth was, he wasn't sure he was ready for any of it. But his choice was made.

He had approached the Androski dozens of times before going through. Getting there and returning to Earth wasn't a

104

problem, it was going through and the uncertainty that followed.

There was one thing he was certain of, though, he had a good crew. Everyone had a job, and with the two extra crew members, it helped Finch feel more at ease.

Although nothing was going to make him one hundred percent relaxed, he took comfort in knowing everyone on board was on the same page.

As he stepped on board the Omni, waving his final good-byes and closing the door, Finch tucked away his insecurities and worries and allowed the excitement to be forefront.

"Life support on," Finch ordered. Already suited up, he placed on his helmet and secured it. Once he saw the others had done the same, he turned on the inter-suit radios. "Androski in range."

"Preparing for entry," Sam said.

"Everyone know what they need to do when we get through the other side?" He received their acknowledgements. Slowly he exhaled through his parted lips. "Here we go."

In those final seconds so much went through Finch's mind. He kept thinking about what Tucker had said after lift-off.

How they had to remember that the Androski was still a wormhole and Einstein theorized wormholes were doorways to other galaxies.

Could the Androski suddenly toss them somewhere else and not to another time? Could they float in some black abyss, unable to return, unable to truly see the Androski to go back through?

It was insane how his mind flipped through the thoughts as his heart raced.

He was okay until that very moment.

But it was too late to go back.

At least he would get to see what it was like going through. The first time they lost all power and life support and the entire crew passed out.

Not this time.

Unless the ship somehow was crushed, Finch would see it all.

They entered.

The second they slipped in the ship went dark.

A beautiful series of bright lights flashed around them. Finch was prepared at the controls, ready to face the large blue planet that would not only block their way but try to suck them into its field.

"Sam, you ready?"

"I'm ready. Five seconds..." Sam counted. "Four, three, Two..."

They emerged.

"Now," Finch ordered.

Sam powered up and almost as if he were on some sort of auto command, Finch veered the ship hurriedly to the left.

But there was no reason to. Nothing was there. No blue planet, just a view of Earth in the distance.

"What the hell?" Tucker said. "Taking off my helmet."

"Where did it go?" Finch asked.

"It's not here," Sam said. "Did we go that far back?" He took off his helmet.

"I see it," Nate said. "There. Forty-five degrees."

Finch turned the ship. Sure enough, he finally saw the planet. It had not settled into the Earth's orbit yet and was still at a distance where it looked no bigger than a soft ball. "Sam, how close was it when you left?"

"Not that close."

"So we came through somewhere between you leaving and where we just left."

Nate chuckled. "That's a span of a hundred and forty years."

"Maybe the ARCS haven't left," Rey suggested.

"If they actually lifted off, we're past that time," Tucker said. "The Big Blue is closer than you think. You can't really see Mars, it's just a speck and that is sixty-million miles away. In your time you couldn't even see the blue. When we left it was approximately thirty million miles away and moving steadily. At first it moved like a bullet. Then it slowed. It took a hundred and forty-five years to travel roughly twenty-nine-and-a-half million miles. That planet right there is well over half the distance. So if I was to make an estimated guess, we went back seventy or eighty years. Half the time frame since Omni left."

"Which means," Finch said, "if the ARCS lifted off as scheduled, they left Earth fifty or so years ago."

"About that," Tucker said.

"Wait," Nate interjected. "I just thought of something. Quinn is eight years off. He has to be."

"What do you mean?" Finch asked.

"Well, he told us we left Earth a hundred and sixty-seven years earlier, right?"

"Right." Finch nodded.

"How can that be?" Nate asked. "He said he and Genesis had been on the new Earth for twenty-five years and four months. He must have miscalculated somewhere how far into the future he was. If he said we arrived at Earth-167. Quinn would have arrived at Earth-142. How can that be?"

Tucker snapped his finger. "You're right. He wouldn't have arrived in any time frame where the Androski wasn't open. He had to have arrived around Earth-150."

"I can imagine the data may have been skewed," Finch said. "Time, weather, I mean they searched for information. In the grand scheme of things what is eight years? A zero written on a piece of paper could have been mistaken for another number."

"Does it make a difference?" Sam asked.

Tucker bobbed his head back and forth. "As far as growth goes, yeah, but I guess not."

"Stop." Rey held up her hand forming a T. "So as not to be confused anymore, and for consistency, we just left Earth, what number?"

Tucker looked at Nate as if to silently agree upon something. "Earth-175. So, we would roughly be around Earth-100 right now, give or take. Meaning right now it's a hundred years after you guys originally left Earth."

"Which means, looking below," Rey said, "it's possible people are still down there, struggling."

"Would they still be alive?" asked Sam.

"Yes," Rey said. "There could be a lot of people down there."

"I agree," said Finch. "Let's orbit. Nate and Freeman, once we get into the atmosphere, focus on the scans as they come in. Look for signs of life, see if you can figure out what is going on, if things have changed. Sam, I need you to go into the navigational system, pull up the coordinates of the ARC launch sites, they're in there. We'll do a fly by when we orbit."

"Roger that, Commander," Sam replied. "Any idea where you want to put us down?"

"We have three states to choose from," Finch said. "We'll take our pick when we see the scans. Hopefully, that intel Quinn found was correct and Wyoming, Colorado, and Utah were barely hit." He glanced over his shoulder. Nate and Tucker hustled to set up their station to monitor, but Rey didn't say anything. She stared out the window. "Rey, are you alright?"

"I'm fine, just…we left to find a new home for those on Earth. We arrived on Earth when everything was over. Somehow, I feel," Rey said, "we're about to land right in the middle of all the hell."

"Sadly," Finch said, "I think you're right."

"Two, three, five…" Nate shook his head. "Too many storms to count in the pacific. But Hawaii is gone, Finch. Not there."

"Seas are insane," Tucker said. "Though not as bad as when we left."

"Still seeing Australia," Nate said. "Nothing on Japan, though. I don't see it. It's gone."

"Keep looking," Finch ordered. "It's darker on this side of the world. It could be the storms. We could have missed it. We're clearing the storms now."

"It's not there," Nate replied.

Finch looked over at Sam and saw his reaction. Sam had closed his eyes, taking in that information. "Sam, are you okay?"

"Yeah. Yeah. Fine." Sam cleared his throat and returned focus to his screen.

"Nate, keep looking. Sam anything on your end with the ARCs?"

"Hunan Province ARC is not there," Sam replied. "We're not close enough to confirm Gansu or Tibet."

"But Hunan is not there?"

"It is not there."

"Well, one ARC got off the ground. Cities? Anyone seeing anything on cities?"

"We can zero on one," Tucker said.

"Do that."

"It's dark," Nate stated. "As you said it's barely morning over here. There are no lights. No sign of power."

"We still have a lot of area to cover," Finch said. "Let's keep checking."

"Quinn said Europe went under first," Rey said. "From what he read that seemed to be the kickoff, so if it's still there, the world is not over. Not yet."

"What difference does it make?" Sam asked. "Can we do anything about it?"

"If there is anyone left down there, yeah we can," Rey said. "We can try. We know there are three safe states. Right now, they may not know that."

"It's a lot of years, Rey," Sam said. "Just saying, a lot of years. Almost a hundred since Tucker and I left. I'm not holding out much hope."

Rey nodded. He had a point. It didn't matter though. They couldn't just say, 'well this is a bust let's hit the Androski again.' No matter how bad it was below, the ship needed to recharge and they had no choice but to land.

SEVENTEEN

The Omni flew on autopilot just as they finished the first orbit. Nate called everyone into the back to show them what he'd figured out with Tucker.

"We have two hours of power," Finch said. "Then we are out. So once we figure out where we are landing, I can turn around."

"You'll be able to turn around shortly," Nate said. "But I needed you guys to be informed first."

A twenty-inch monitor was before him and on it was a still image of the United States. "This is where we are," Nate explained. "No cloud formation and we have a beautiful image. Now..." In the corner another image appeared. "This is Earth when Omni left. I call it Earth Zero."

The images then appeared side by side.

"You can clearly see the difference." Nate pointed. "Florida is no longer half gone. Like it was when we left. You can see the east coast is starting to expand and the southern west coast is slowly being swallowed, opening Nevada up to prime beach front property. Next image..." His finger clicked and another image appeared. He moved it to the right so that the current United States image was center. "This image is Earth one-seventy-five. One hundred and seventy-five years after we left. Big difference from Earth Zero." He pointed to the image on the left. "But...If you

111

look…" A few keystrokes and Earth-175 turned into an out-line, and using his finger Nate slid it over Earth-100, the time where they were now.

"Look at that, Sam," Tucker said. "He has touch screen."

Nate smiled. "You're funny. If you look at this, it's about halfway to where we are now at Earth-100, right here and now. Therefore, nothing occurred overnight, which is a good thing and the reason that a lot of buildings remain. Had the shift or whatever occurred over the course of one year, no one would have been able to withstand it."

"How does it look now as far as life and so forth?" Finch asked.

"There are segments of the country that look to me as totally overgrown, not the same at all. I'd say abandoned at least for twenty-five years."

Finch rubbed his chin. "Anywhere to land?"

"Actually, yes," Nate answered. "Tucker?"

"You told us about the Wyoming, Utah, Colorado stuff so we concentrated on there," he said. "Hey, Sam, watch as I pinch the screen and enlarge."

"You're an ass," Sam replied.

Tucker enlarged the map of Earth Zero. "This is the area we focused on. And this is how it looks now…" He switched images to the same enlargement of the three states. "There's lots and lots of overgrown areas. But look at this area north of Fort Collins…" He zoomed in even more. "There's not a lot, but there, a farm. Unlike anything else in the area. Judging by this image, this farm is maintained. Small but maintained. Someone is there."

"And you're absolutely sure," Finch said, "it isn't aban-doned."

"It could be now, but I've been a farm boy my entire life. This farm has upkeep. It looks too perfect on this image."

"Good." Finch folded his arms. "We have a destination. Sam, let's turn the ship around. Nate, find us an area near there big enough to land," he said. "Let's get on the ground and find out what's going on."

Just like the sun that traveled east to west, the density of overgrowth lessened. Although, highly populated areas all around the country appeared to be the worst. Cities had been abandoned in the wake of disasters such as earthquakes, hurricanes, tornados, and other events. Disasters with a magnitude no one could have ever predicted.

Most highways appeared to still be intact. From the air they looked better than on the ground. The six-lane road South College Avenue served as a landing strip for the Omni. For the most part it was smooth. The few cracks that spouted growing weeds were barely felt under the massive weight of the vessel.

Finch pulled the Omni into a strip mall parking lot. The few cars that remained were out of the way. It was open, with very few trees and plenty of ultraviolet light.

There were no signs of people, nor did it look like anyone had been there for a long time.

Tucker immediately did what he had done when the Lola landed. He checked out the sun, estimated the time and set his watch.

It wasn't early, in fact, by his estimate it was mid-afternoon. It didn't leave much time for any charging the ship could do.

While Sam and Finch prepared the buggy, and Nate transferred his map images to a tablet, Rey and Tucker walked the strip mall and looked in the stores.

The entire place was weather worn. The bricks were cracked and chipped, the paint on the edges of windows and doors, peeling. Some of the signs had fallen and most of the windows were shattered, more than likely from age and the elements.

A red four-door sedan was parked just outside of the first shop, a pizza joint.

The car was parked across two spots and the hood was open. Inside the engine block a garden had started to grow. The doors were open; nothing or no one was inside.

"Wonder if they broke down," Tucker said, peeking inside. "Hope they got a ride."

"I don't understand. What happened in this town?" said Rey. "I mean, it doesn't look like earthquake damage."

"No, it doesn't. Or a tornado or freak flood." Tucker pulled out his small, rectangular light and walked to the wide-open pizza shop window. He shone the light in, moving it left to right before stepping over the window edge and going inside.

He held out his hand to Rey. "Watch your step."

She took his hand as a guide, until she stepped into the restaurant.

It was a typical strip mall outlet. The restaurant was long and narrow. Ten feet into the place on the left was a counter that ran most of the length of the restaurant. A cash register sat at the beginning of it, plexiglass shields hanging down to the counter. Behind it were pizza ovens.

The décor, from what Tucker could tell in the dim light, was dated. Black-and-white tiles covered the floor. The bottom half of the walls were some sort of wood and above the chair railings were mirrors, probably there to give the illusion that the place was bigger than it was.

Weeds grew from the linoleum floor and crept up the counter by the register. A result of seed and pollen blowing in through the open windows. Only a few sections of the mirrors were broken.

"No one left in a hurry," said Tucker.

"Why do you say that?"

"Well, everything is clean. No plates, food left out. I mean that area with the sneeze guard looks like where they put the pizza out for people to pick a slice. Nothing is there. This place was closed."

"In the back, look at the chairs."

Tucker moved the light and noticed two tables were disturbed. One had been turned over on its side with the flat side of the table facing out, and the chairs were toppled. "What the heck?" He stepped toward the table.

"What is it?" Rey asked.

Tucker ran his fingers over the table. "Bullet holes."

"Someone hid behind the table?" Rey asked.

"Looks that way." Tucker walked behind it. "No blood on the wall."

"How about bodies."

"If there were bodies, there wouldn't be anything left. I mean those windows busted out from time. Over time the seal breaks, that takes a few decades."

"What about clothing?" Rey questioned.

"Maybe."

"Well, check."

"Check for bodies?" Tucker asked.

"Yes."

"Fine." He walked around the table. "This is odd. No bodies but..."

"What is it?" Rey asked, joining him. "What do you got?"

Tucker lifted a bracelet of sorts. A black plastic band. He bent down and grabbed another. "Don't these look like those exercise bracelets?"

"Yeah, they do." Rey took one.

"Who the heck gets shot at and leaves their exercise bracelets behind?"

Rey examined it, running her fingers along the side. After doing that, three small green lights lit up on the edge. "Heck of a battery."

"That is really strange." Tucker took it, looked at it again, and placed both in the small bag he carried over his shoulder. "Bullet holes, exercise bracelets..."

"And a bunny."

"What?"

Rey bent down and lifted a rag doll style toy bunny from the floor. It was nearly buried beneath dirt and dust. She cleaned it off by hitting it a few times on the table's edge. "This belonged to a child. God, I hope they weren't shot."

"Why would there be a shoot-out here?" Tucker questioned, more so thinking out loud. "This doesn't make sense."

"A robbery or someone looting, perhaps?"

"I don't think so. What would someone loot?"

"Food. Money," Rey suggested.

"Exactly." Tucker pointed the light at the front. "Register is fine. Soda case still has soda, chips are still there. If they're looting for food, why not take those?" Tucker, with the light in hand, stepped back, shining it around. He paused when he heard a faint mechanical whirling. It was short and soft. "Rey, did you hear that?"

"Hear what?"

"I guess not." He moved slowly counterclockwise, shining the light, and just as he faced the rear corner, he saw it.

There was a door there, right in the back of the restaurant. It probably led to a back room. It was a swinging door, no knob, with a small square window near the top.

It was there in that window it appeared.

A red dot of light. Small and round. The sight of it was so startling to Tucker, he not only jumped, he let out a small shriek.

"What?" Rey asked. "You scared me."

"That." Tucker pointed.

"What? What am I looking at?"

He lowered his hand. "It was there. It's gone."

"What was it?"

"I don't know." Tucker moved toward that door. "I'm gonna find out. I saw a demon."

Rey snorted a laugh. "I'm sorry, a demon?"

"Okay not a demon, but I swear it was a red eye like some horror movie," Tucker said.

"Maybe it was your light reflecting off of something."

"Maybe," Tucker said. "I'm going to find out."

"Tucker. Rey," Finch called out.

Tucker was already on heightened nerves and Finch's call just made him jump again.

"What the hell is the matter with you?" Rey asked.

"I wasn't expecting him to call our names." Tucker looked to the front of the restaurant. Finch stood there.

"You guys alright?" Finch asked.

Rey answered, "Yeah, we're fine. Tucker saw a demon."

"Tucker saw a what?" Finch asked.

"Oh, stop," Tucker said. "I just saw something weird."

"The buggy is ready to go." Finch pointed back. "It's getting late so if we want to find that farm, we need to get a move on."

"Commander?" Tucker walked toward him. "Can we not?"

"I'm sorry." Finch titled his head. "You spotted the farm. You were the one that told us about it. Why are we not looking for it?"

"We will," Tucker explained. "It just that…it's getting late. When we find the farm, we'll find the farmer, hopefully. We need more time than just to say howdy and turn back here to the ship. Let's make camp. I think not only would we do better finding the farm when we have a whole day ahead of us, but we need to check out this town."

"He's right," Rey said.

"What's going on?" Finch asked.

Tucker shook his head. "I don't know. But something. We have an empty town. Very few cars. No damage other than what the passing of time would do. So no natural disasters here. There are bullet holes in here. A shoot-out in a pizza place. Food is still everywhere. It doesn't make sense. This is just one place. There are a lot more buildings just around here to check out. I think if we're piecing together what happened to Earth between Earth Zero and Earth-175, we need to examine what happened in his town."

"Show him what you found," Rey said.

Tucker reached into his shoulder bag and pulled out one of the bracelets. "Buried in the dust on the floor behind the table. A table, mind you, set up as a shield from bullets."

"A fitness bracelet?" Finch examined it.

"Strange, isn't it?" Tucker asked.

"It is." Finch returned it. "Alright, we'll set up camp and do some exploring. It's not like we're in a rush."

"Thank you," said Tucker.

Finch nodded his acknowledgement and turned. He paused and looked back. "Are you two coming to help set up camp?"

Rey glanced up to Tucker. "Did you want to check out the demon thing first?"

Tucker looked behind him to the door. "Nah, we can come back and see. Let's help set up camp."

The three of them left the pizza shop, but not before Tucker looked back at that door just one more time.

EIGHTEEN

Something about Tucker's sudden switch from carefree to concerned put Finch on high alert. Tucker was an intelligent man with what Finch believed was a lot of common sense. When he suddenly stopped sightseeing, Finch felt Tucker had a gut instinct about something. He wasn't mentioning anything, but it was there. Finch took no chances.

Unlike when they landed on Earth-175, Finch set up security measures before they left to explore. Placing the security poles in four points around the ship, Finch initiated the electric perimeter and alarm.

He'd leave it up all night while they slept too.

Even though the town seemed dead and not a soul was around, that wasn't to say there weren't animals.

Rules were set.

They went into the same area together. They could check buildings in teams.

No one said anything to Finch at first, they just did what was told until he gave his talk before going out.

"We will take one buggy, slow moving," Finch said. "Tucker and Sam, I want you on point. I'll follow behind, Nate and Rey in the buggy." He checked the clip in his pistol.

"Um, Finch?" Nate asked. "What gives?"

"I'm sorry," Finch replied. "What do you mean?"

"Well, no one is around. It's almost as if you're expecting us to be ambushed."

"He's being proactive," Rey said. "It's very strange around here and it's not like where we were before. We didn't know it was inhabited. This is Earth not long after things really fell apart, so there could be people around."

Sam added, "There's a farm. So we know there is someone."

"I think it's smart," Tucker said. "Something doesn't feel right around here. I don't know what it is."

"Demons," Sam said. "Demons with red eyes."

Tucker shot a glance to Rey. "Did you say something to him?"

"Not making fun, I swear." Rey held up her hand. "I was telling him. That's all."

"Well, I saw something. It was there one second, the next it was gone," Tucker said.

Nate suggested, "Maybe your flashlight reflected off an animal's eyes."

"Big animal," Tucker replied.

"It could have been a racoon on a shelf or something," Nate said.

Tucker nodded. "You know what? That actually sounds plausible."

"In any event," Finch said, "we roll out as a team, staying close. We can hit these stores in the strip mall when we get back." He pointed. "Right now, let's cross that road and check out those houses. I saw them when we flew over."

"What are we looking for?" Sam asked.

"Anything and everything," Finch replied. "There has to be a paper trail. A time stamp of events. Something."

"Junk drawers," Rey said. "Almost every kitchen has a junk drawer. Look there, behind the fridge, places mail could end up."

Tucker shook his head. "There is no mail. I mean, there is and isn't. The post office was no more when I was thirteen. There are independent letter companies, or were, but not like when you guys were on Earth."

"Aw," Nate said. "My friend was a mail carrier."

Tucker shrugged. "It wasn't profitable."

"That makes sense," Rey said.

"Then something else..." Finch instructed. "Just find dates and any info you can. This town was not hit with any major disasters. It's still standing. Let's see if we can find out why there are no signs of life."

They left the parking lot and the ship, crossing over the six-lane road to a side street that nestled between another strip mall and a convenience store.

At the end of the block, just before the residential area, was a tiny building that housed two eateries. Like twin restaurants, one on the left the other on the right. The big front windows of both restaurants were broken. Both had an outdoor patio. The railings were overgrown with weeds and not a single outdoor table was out.

As they started to pass, Tucker lifted his hand for Nate to stop.

"Do you see something?" Finch asked.

Tucker walked to his left and to the restaurant and stood there for a second. He reached out and grabbed something, then returned to the buggy.

"What is it?" Finch asked.

"Was a sign," Tucker replied. "They had it in plastic too, but it's really faded, probably from the sun. Can't make it out." He gave it to Finch.

"A sign on the door. The place was probably closed. I'll hold on to it." He opened a case in the back of the buggy, placed it inside, and closed it again.

He then signaled for them to continue.

The road curved around into the residential area. An apartment complex sat on one side of the road and houses on the other. They were quaint houses, all frame, and most were one story. They were all set up the same: a wide driveway and small front laws that had long since grown over.

The street was cracked as roots from the trees made their way through.

"Be careful inside," Finch instructed. "Watch your step, these houses may not be the sturdiest right now." He looked at his watch. "Tucker time has us at four p.m. Let's do a few houses, get what we can, head back to camp and examine our findings."

There were five houses on that small bend and they would be their starting point.

Rey grabbed the empty gear bag and placed the strap over her shoulder as she, Finch, and Nate walked to the first house. Even staying on the pathway to the house was difficult to get to with all the overgrowth.

Finch walked ahead to the front door and turned the knob. "It's not locked." He pushed on it, but it didn't open. Stepping back, he examined the archway.

"Is something blocking it?" Nate asked.

"No, I think it's just warped." He gave it a couple of shoves with his shoulder, and it budged enough for him to put his head inside. "Not blocked. It's the floor." He kept at it a few more times, opening it enough for them to slip in. "Watch your step, the hardwood floors are lifted."

Nate passed inside first, with Rey behind him.

She waited for Finch to enter. The front door brought them straight into the living room. It was a simple layout, the kitchen right off the living room and a small dinette area in the corner.

The floor was lifted in so many spots; at one time it was probably beautiful. The sofa looked as if insects or something had eaten it. More than likely it was just the passing of time causing it to fall apart.

"Finch?" Rey asked. "Why are the windows here not all broken?"

"Probably because they're better windows. Windows loosen over time and a good wind can take them out. These are sturdier, I would think."

"Pictures," Nate said.

Finch and Rey looked at him questioningly.

He walked across the living room to the fireplace and the mantle. "There are pictures here."

"Okay," Finch said, not quite understanding where he was going.

"It's a well-known fact that if someone is leaving home for good, they take personal items over anything else."

"Unless they left in a rush," Rey said. "Maybe there was a threat of something happening and they just ran. I didn't see a car in the driveway."

"Evacuation would give them enough time to take photographs," Finch added. "We should check the garage after we leave."

"It could have been a biological event like what happened with my family," Nat said. "Maybe something like that happened here."

"We'll find out," replied Finch. "Nate, look around this room. Check the closets. Rey, you have the kitchen and I'll head to the bedrooms. Call out either of you if you run into any problems."

"It's a little house," Rey said. "I think we're good."

Nate stayed in the living room and Rey went to the kitchen. It wasn't very wide. It was long and a vine-like mold crept up over the walls. There were dishes in the sink with some sort of crust growing over them. Her first instincts were to open the cabinets. There weren't that many, and it wouldn't take long. She opened the first one to find a set of dishes and cups, the next was exactly the same. She thought it strange and opened the wide one. A red piece of tape ran vertically down the center. Each side had boxed and canned goods.

Whoever was there left and didn't take food. To Rey that was strange.

Checking drawers would be just as easy. The first one she opened was next to the dishwasher. It contained serving utensils, the next one aluminum foil.

Nothing else.

She shuffled over to the first row of drawers by the wall and started on them.

Top draw was silverware, under that...silverware.

She tilted her head in confusion, then pulled open every drawer. Out of everything, and more odd than them not having a junk drawer were the two identical silverware drawers.

"Finch?" she called out.

"Yeah," he answered from the back of the house.

She left the kitchen, turned right immediately and walked down the short hall. He was in the last room to the right, standing at a dresser. "Hey," she said.

"Hey, what's up?"

"I saw something strange."

"Me too."

"Not only do they not have a junk drawer..."

"Rey." He chuckled. "Not everyone has a junk drawer. I didn't," Finch said.

"I think you're the only one. Anyhow, they have two sets of dishes, two sets of silverware...like maybe they took a tenant. It's just a really small house to do that."

"I'm trying to figure that out," Finch replied. "Everything in here was boxed up. Like the person died or something."

"Maybe they were moving in."

"I don't think so." Finch lifted up a wallet. It was covered in a thick layer of dirt. He flipped it open and showed Rey. "Look at the license."

"William Kramer...thirty-two," Rey said. "What about him?"

"Look at the state on the license."

"Virginia. I would say a relative, but why divide everything up?"

"I think he died," Finch said. "They were packing up his stuff whenever what happened, happened. It's just strange that someone from Virginia would be sharing a tiny two-bedroom house with someone all the way in Colorado."

"An internet love affair?" Rey guessed.

Finch laughed. "You're funny."

"Hey, guys." Nate poked his head into the room. "Check this out." He handed Finch an envelope. "It's a letter. No stamp, but like Tucker said, some weird courier name."

"Where did you find it?" Rey asked.

"Oh, they had a junk drawer in the dining-room buffet table."

"Damn it," Rey said. "Who does that? Who has a junk drawer in the dining room?"

126

Finish looked at the letter. "It's pretty preserved."

"It was in the drawer pretty good," Nate said. "Look at the date. Forty-five years after we left. Twenty years after Tucker and Sam left, five years before the ARCs."

"What is it?" Rey asked. "What does it say?"

"It gives us the answer to the out-of-state roommate," Finch replied. "The letter is from…something called the Federal Relocation Program. William Kramer was moved here by the government." Finch handed her the letter. "And these folks had no choice but to take him in."

It didn't look it from the outside, but Tucker thought it was a really cool house. It was the only one that was two stories, but he wouldn't have called it that. The second floor was only six stairs up. It was more like a split level.

Sam and Tucker had to enter through the back. The front door wouldn't open no matter how hard they pushed. The sliding glass doors that led to the patio were broken and they just walked in.

The house was a mess. Furniture was broken, some overturned, nature had crept up everywhere and the carpet had turned into a garden.

The cathedral ceilings were riddled with holes and there was water damage in the living room from the broken window on the ceiling.

At one time, Tucker was sure it was the best house on the block. He imagined the family had lots of gatherings; the backyard was set up for it.

He made a comment to Sam that he wouldn't swim in the pool. It looked like a swamp and they got a good chuckle out of it.

It wasn't what Tucker expected to walk into. It was completely opposite from the first house they entered. That one was small, a single-story ranch style. It looked like a starter home for a young couple. They had a baby, a deduction that was pretty easy once they saw the crib.

The first house left in a hurry. Nothing was disturbed, food was still in the cabinets, and the trash was still in the can.

He'd gathered some stuff from the junk drawer in the dining room of that house, a few pictures, and a journal.

Not much else, there wasn't that much to get at the first house.

It was boring.

No one was there. No remains of bodies or a car. They left.

But the split-level house was a whole other ball game.

There was a car in the driveway. The house was in disarray, like some huge brawl broke out before everything happened.

The front door was not only bolted, but the reason that Sam and Tucker couldn't get in was because it had a security bar on it.

Even though the walls exhibited mold and growth, Tucker didn't see any blood or any bodies there.

The people left. Not only that, they took food.

The cabinets in the kitchen were bare and the doors to the cabinets had been left open.

While Sam examined the first floor further, Tucker walked up those six steps to the upper level.

Three bedrooms.

The house looked smaller on the outside than it did on the inside.

He paused at the first bedroom and looked at the slightly open door.

It was damaged.

When Tucker saw that door, he immediately thought about his dorm roommate in college. A young, angry man who would emotionally get out of control when he drank. One night that college roommate got into a fight with his girlfriend and in his alcohol-induced rage, punched the door, putting an indentation and slight crack in it.

The door to the bedroom in the home had a similar mark.

Tucker ran his fingers over the hole, then pushed the door open.

The bed was overturned; posters that at one time hung on the walls dangled and were partially deteriorated.

"What the hell happened here?" Tucker said out loud to himself.

The damage made as much sense to him as the bullet-riddled table in the pizza parlor.

One house peace, the second chaos.

He stepped further into the room and reached for a dresser drawer. It took some struggling to open it, but when he did he saw clothes.

The closet was open and clothes, still on hangers, were piled on the floor.

"Tuck." Sam rushed into the room.

Tucker spun around. "You scared me."

"You have to see this."

"Did you find something?" Tucker asked.

"Yeah, and it makes no sense."

"Sam, this entire house makes no sense," Tucker said. "Makes me think of those old cop shows where the police come in and raid a place, turning it upside down."

"You might not be far off with that." Sam led him down the six steps and to the front door. The security bar that kept it closed was off to the side and Sam opened it. "I decided to see if there was another car in the garage." Sam walked outside and turned right to the garage that was attached to the house. The door was open.

Tucker saw two cars in there, parked side by side. "They had three cars?"

"No. I thought that when I walked in here..." Sam said. "I thought, wow, not only is this a clean garage, but small. Short, you know, they couldn't park that SUV on the driveway in there."

"No, they could not."

"I didn't see it at first when I opened the garage door but...come here." He walked down the side of the car to the back wall. "Look."

"What the hell?" Tucker blurted out when he saw there was a huge hole, at least four foot around, in the back wall.

"Yeah. And it doesn't go to the backyard." Sam lifted his flashlight and shone it in. "It's hollow."

"It's a room," Tucker said. He pulled out his rectangular LED light and with it lit he climbed through. "Sam, get in here."

The light was bright enough to illuminate the entire area.

It was long and narrow. There were blankets and cots, food scattered about.

"People lived back here," Tucker said. "It's a hidden room."

"That hole...that hole, they either escaped..." Sam said.

"Or someone pulled them out."

"Tuck, why build a hidden room in the garage?"

"I think the better question should be," Tucker said, "what were they hiding from?"

NINETEEN

It wasn't quiet when it should have been. Nate couldn't quite place the sound. It wasn't an animal or human, it was closer to a click and hum. But it was faint and just when he thought he heard it, it was gone. More than likely it was Tucker and Sam.

It started after dinner when they were getting ready to settle down for the evening. Right after Tucker and Sam took off for a walk, despite Finch's advice to stay put.

Though they did check in every five minutes by radio.

Nate had cooked the meal. He'd used the fresh vegetables from Quinn, the preserved chicken breasts, and made a nice stir fry, without stir frying it.

Everyone enjoyed it.

Finch had suggested taking a break after dinner. Take time for everyone to clear their minds after the search, and then once they were refreshed they could revisit and discus.

Rey had set up the fire pan, a miniature version of a fire pit, and had a small fire going. She sat on a cushion and next to her was the gear bag. It was open and she shuffled through items.

Nate pulled up his chair. He looked at Finch, who kicked back. "Anything from them?"

"They are due to radio in a few."

"Do we have to wait?" Rey asked. "I came up with some interesting things."

"Like?" Finch asked.

"Like, there wasn't much in the first house. But our second one..." Rey said. "Someone in that house went on the ARC."

"What?" Finch sat up, leaning forward. "Why didn't you say anything earlier?"

"Well, it was such a good find," Rey said. "I wanted to tell everyone all at once. This person was selected really early, too." She reached into the bag and pulled out a frame. "His mom was proud. Apparently, he was selected for his ongoing work in robotics."

"Interesting." Finch took the frame. "I didn't realize that was one of the categories."

"It was fifty years after our time," Nate said. "A lot could have changed."

"Very true. So anything else?" Finch asked.

"You mean like, that wasn't enough?" Rey asked.

"I didn't say that, I was just..."

"Apparently, there weren't any natural disasters. From the looks of the stores," Nate said. "They closed down. So, that tells us something happened here."

"No shit," snapped Rey.

"What is that about?" Finch questioned. "Why the bad mood?"

"I'm pissed, we're supposed to share what we found and put our heads together. Where are they?" Rey said. "Not here."

"They'll be here soon. We can talk without them."

"Just that we'll have to repeat it," Rey said.

"She has a point," Nate agreed.

"Fine." Finch lifted the radio. "Tucker. Come in. Are you guys coming back any time soon?"

"On our way, Commander," Tucker replied. "We found something."

"Roger that, see you soon." Finch glanced at Rey.

Nate saw it; she didn't look happy.

"What is it now?" Finch asked her.

"Now, everything they say is going to be important, like ours isn't."

Finch laughed. "Rey, what is wrong with you tonight? Have some of that Quinn wine. It's good stuff, relax."

"Speaking of Quinn," Nate said. "Did he ever give us any definite indication of when things happened? Like the big stuff."

"Obviously, sometime after right now," Finch said. "I just wish we knew when we were."

Rey raised her hand and spoke cheerfully. "I found a loaf of bread today."

Finch and Nate just looked at her.

"It really wasn't a loaf of bread, more a lump of something hard, green, and unknown."

They still stared at her as if she were nuts.

"I was kind of shocked it was that bad," Rey said. "The Dawsons..."

"Who?" Finch asked.

"Second house, they were they Dawsons," Rey replied. "The name on the letter."

"Oh." Finch nodded.

"Anyhow, the Dawsons had been storing food. I mean, hiding it for some reason, maybe there was a run on things. They had these gray plastic storage bins, the type I used to store my Christmas decorations. Why they didn't stick it in a freezer, I don't know."

"Maybe," Finch said. "If they were hiding it, it would be seen."

"Good point."

"Where is this going?" Nate asked.

"I'm getting there. I was going to wait," Rey said, "until Tucker and Sam got back, but I want to break the news first in case they found it out."

"What news?" Nate asked. "That bread stored in gray plastic container turns into a lump of something?"

"Sealed container. That's important," Rey said.

Finch shook his head. "Okay, I am going to let you roll, because, obviously, you are building to something big."

"I am," Rey said. "The sealed container allowed the plastic wrapping over the bread to be in good condition and…let me see the sell-by date. That sell by year was five years after the letter Nate found. Which also let me know that Tucker was off by twenty-five years. If we go by the intervals of the Androski, the date on the letter, and condition of the town, we are not on Earth one hundred, we are only seventy-five years in the future after we left. Because there is no way this town has been empty for fifty years."

"Oh my God," Finch said. "That is amazing. That really is amazing."

"It is," Nate stated. "Although I'm pretty sure there was a shorter way to say it."

Rey was going to say something but looked beyond Nate.

Tucker and Sam were returning, walking at a quick pace to the camp.

Finch stood. "Everything alright?" he asked.

"Yeah." Tucker nodded. "It's been an eventful evening."

"It has," Finch said. "Rey just told us she figured out when we are. In a pretty impressive way, too."

"From a loaf of bread," Rey said. "We're seventy-five years post-Omni."

"Wow, really?" Tucker asked. "Makes what we found even more disheartening."

"What did you find?" Finch questioned.

Again, Tucker looked at Sam.

Sam answered, "We found out...what happened in this town."

"If we take the solar buggy," Finch said, "we're not going to be able to go to the farm tomorrow. It will use all the power and we'll spend the day recharging."

"One more day won't hurt," Tucker replied. "The farm will still be there, it gives us time to figure things out here, and still time to catch the Androski. By the size of it, it's not closing soon."

Finch asked, "Is it that far to walk?"

"We were gone two hours," Tucker replied. "One lead led to another."

"I'm not going to like where this is going, am I?" Finch questioned.

"It gives answers," Tucker replied. "But not all."

Before all five of them loaded into the buggy, Tucker and Sam retrieved the larger version of their pocket LED lights, both eighteen inches wide.

Sam attached one to the top of the buggy. It lit up the road better than any headlight system could do.

They didn't drive far or for too long.

Tucker told them how he and Sam had just started walking when it dawned on them to check out a specific location.

Absolutely nothing they saw gave an indication to what they would find.

They drove through a residential area until they arrived and stopped at the rear entrance to the high school.

"Keep in mind it was still light when we first walked here," Tucker explained.

"We weren't even going to stop," added Sam. "We walked right by it."

"That's when we noticed the entire area north of the school," Tucker said. "On this side of the road...it was flattened. Gone. But it wasn't a field and trees like we thought. There had been all kinds of buildings and stuff here. When we walked through we saw wood sticking out of the ground, chimneys, you name it."

"We walked up for two blocks, maybe three," Sam said. "Everything was gone. It was another block before we realized it wasn't like a gas explosion, but that the buildings had been flattened on purpose. There is a one-block section of nothing but rubble. Knocked down and pushed aside."

"Did you figure out why?" Finch asked.

"We did, which led us to here first." Sam pointed to the school grounds, then drove onto the property.

Tucker leaned forward from the back seat. "At first we wondered why they didn't tear this down."

"They did, sort of," Sam said. "The school buildings are all gone."

"But not the stadium," Tucker said.

They drove a little closer and when they did, they saw several dump trucks parked outside the stadium, along with a crane.

"Looks like they were going to tear this down," Finch said.

"That's what we thought too," Tucker replied.

136

Sam drove directly to the gate of the stadium. "Until we went inside."

Rey glanced at Tucker. "Why do I think I know where this is going?"

The buggy stopped and they all stepped out.

Sam left the one light on the vehicle and Tucker turned on the other, leading Finch, Rey, and Nate inside.

There was no particular smell that stood out, and it was too dark to see after they walked through the gate.

Finch felt the softness under his feet, and occasionally the snap of a twig. The ground and galleys of the stadium were overgrown.

The light was exceptionally bright but it was one directional, illuminating a good walking path and showing the opening to the actual field.

And then a few rows into the stadium seating, the light hit a wall. The wall started before the field and was at least twenty feet high.

"Fort Collins wasn't a small town," Sam said. "A hundred thousand or so people lived here. Not a major metropolis, but no village either."

"So where did everyone go?" Nate asked.

"A lot right here," Sam said.

"What were they trying to build in here?" Rey asked.

"They weren't building anything," Sam explained. "That's a wall of bodies."

Rey spun to Sam. "You're kidding me."

"It's dark, but in the day you can clearly see," Sam said. "The ones on the bottom are in bags, merely clothing of the dead now on top. Decay, time, turned the bodies into dust. The ones in the bags not exposed are just bones now."

"Jesus." Nate stepped forward. "Is this the whole city?"

Tucker shook his head. "No, something happened and they never finished."

"Finished what?" Nate asked.

"Burning them," Tucker answered. "I wish you could see right now. It's tough but tomorrow, you can. Out where they tore down the buildings, when you get closer, you can see there are three pits. Nothing ever grew in them because they must have burned bodies in there for a while. The ground is dead."

It wasn't something Finch looked forward to, but knew he had to see.

Perhaps in the light of day they could discover what happened to the people of Fort Collins and maybe learn if it happened everywhere.

Was that why the world was completely grown over? Had the human race faced another extinction event that beat the planetary event to the punch? And when Planet X slid into its orbit, the damage and destruction was, in turn, just part of the evolution for Earth?

One thing was clear to Finch, what had occurred in Fort Collins didn't kill everyone. Some organization had been left standing long enough to collect the bodies.

TWENTY

The next day, while Rey and Nate went on a data search, Finch went back to the high school. Since the buggy had to charge for eight hours, they walked. It was almost two miles, but the temperature wasn't too hot and a slight breeze came in from the west.

Usually, Finch didn't think twice about weather, he was always under the belief there was nothing that could be done about it. Yet, when they first arrived in the future, it seemed the weather had it out for the crew of Omni-4 and he was no longer taking it for granted. He'd be more aware of any changes. Planet X, even at a distance was already wreaking its havoc.

Was it necessary for him to go to the school and the area where they'd burned bodies? Yes.

He had to see for himself.

"The light of day makes everything clearer," his mother used to say. And it held true when Finch stepped into that stadium.

When Tucker and Sam entered the day before it was still somewhat light. Nothing like it was when Finch got his second glance.

The clear sky and bright sun truly showed the massive amount of human devastation.

Nothing remained of the bodies that made up the top third of the mound. The ones on the outer areas were also nothing more than rags of clothing. He assumed the mound was only being held up by the bodies on the inside.

They were skeletons. He guessed tens of thousands.

What a grand movement it had to have been to bring those bodies into the stadium. Apparently, they were dead when they were brought in. Loaded into trucks and lifted by a crane like some sort of game found in an arcade.

Finch had once read a fiction novel which depicted something terribly similar to what he was seeing. He dismissed it as farfetched and beyond the suspension of disbelief, until he saw it firsthand.

There was nothing in the stadium or around it to indicate what had happened that caused such a massive amount of death.

It happened fast.

It had to.

To accumulate that many bodies, and for them to pile so high that it got ahead of those collecting them, whatever caused the event occurred in weeks, if not days.

His mind went immediately to Nate.

Nate lost his father, his mother, and daughter in a freak natural disaster. The type that decades earlier had been called rare, yet, when it happened with Nate, they were commonplace.

A limnic eruption occurred in the small town where Nate's family lived.

An eruption that wasn't volcanic. They happened when CO_2 erupted from deep in a lake causing a toxic cloud that killed everyone and anything alive instantly.

Finch thought of that. There was a small lake in Fort Collins, but was it big enough to cause that much death?

Nate's family lived in a town of three thousand. Fort Collins was bigger, much bigger.

It had to be something like that.

Unless it was an illness. A virus perhaps that swept through town.

Something like that would be worldwide and, hopefully, Rey and Nate could find answers.

As he looked upon the huge number of bodies, he wondered if Earth was just doomed to die. Even though they went as far as one hundred and seventy-five years into the future, was it truly done?

Had nature decided mankind wasn't worth having and was doing everything possible to rid the planet of the human disease, much like the body fought infection.

There were no answers at the stadium, nor were there any answers when Finch visited the areas where they'd burned bodies in huge pits.

Nothing remained in those pits.

The fires had burned so hot and with so much intensity, the ground was charred.

Blackened like charcoal.

It was depressing to think of that large loss of life.

The only consolation Finch found was knowing somehow, someway, the people of Fort Collins died fast. They suffered less than the rest of the world that was crushed in earthquakes, burned by volcanoes, or had starved to death.

Still, in the back of his mind he needed to know why. He couldn't accept that they all just died, that someone or some organization just collected bodies.

The answers were there.

They just had to find them.

"How do a hundred thousand people die all at once?" Rey spoke her thoughts out loud as she walked with Nate.

"They could have died over the course of weeks, too."

"But how?"

"Illness, chemical accident maybe," he said. "Attack."

"Is there a bomb that could do this?"

"Yeah, a thermobaric bomb, but there's still going to be damage," he said. "Thermobarics suck all the air out with a highly intense bomb, but it leaves tops of buildings charred."

"It's just strange, like watching a movie. It's not real because it's not affecting us."

"What if it could?" Nate paused in his walking. "What if whatever killed these people is still around?"

"Fuck."

"Yep."

They walked across the small parking lot to the urgent care. "This," he said, "should give us answers as to what it isn't. Or even what it is."

Like most business the windows were gone, and they climbed through the busted doorway.

"Okay, so…" Rey looked around. "Either they had the most diligent staff or nothing happened. I've seen more chaos first day of shingles vaccines."

Nate chuckled at her and walked behind the check-in counter.

"I'll head to the back," Rey told him.

Other than the typical 'things grew over time' look, it was evident the waiting room of the urgent care had been left impeccable. Nothing was out of order.

She turned on her flashlight and walked down the hall toward the examining rooms. The doors were open and each room that she passed looked the same. Nothing was out of order at all. "Anything?" she called out.

"No paper trail," Nate replied. "They must have done everything on the computer."

There were three doors in that hallway that weren't wide open: the men's room, the ladies' room, and another room labelled 'diagnostics.'

Rey figured it had to be the imaging room for X-rays, but she didn't see that telltale radiation warning symbol.

She turned the knob and pushed the door open slowly, shining her light inside.

There were no windows and the room acted like a tomb; it had been completely sealed off and perfectly preserved. There were no plants or other growth in view. Even the floor felt smooth.

From what she could see there were no large X-ray machines. There was a counter with what looked like lab equipment on top. A rack with test tubes sat next to the sink.

She kicked the stopper on the door to hold it open and walked to the counter.

There were three tubes in the rack; the substance inside looked like dust and she lifted one, shining the light on it to see a date.

It fell in the same time frame as the bread.

Useless, she thought. They needed to go to the hospital and look there. Obviously, no one had gone to the urgent care for whatever ailed the population into death.

Rey inched down, shining her light around the room. There was absolutely nothing significant there. When she took a step to turn, her foot caught it. The tip of her shoe connected with the hard object and she heard it move across the floor and hit something.

What was it?

Bringing her flashlight beam down, she slowly moved it across the floor and when the light hit the object, Rey, so startled, screamed.

She backed up, spun around, and bolted, screaming again when she slammed into Nate.

"What is it? What happened? What's wrong?"

"There..." Rey caught her breath. "Sorry, it scared me."

"What?"

"There's a head."

"A head?"

"A head," Rey said. "It was on the floor, I kicked it by accident."

"That would be impossible."

"See for yourself." Rey pointed, then grabbed onto his arm, pulling him in.

Both of their flashlights gave sufficient lighting and without the element of surprise, Rey got a better look at it.

It definitely wasn't a human head.

Nate crouched down, then lifted it. "It's heavy. Let's take this out front so we can see it in the light."

Rey nodded, waited for Nate to walk by her, and then she followed him down the hall into the reception area.

It was a head and partial neck and it balanced well when Nate set it on the counter. It reminded Rey of a mannequin head in a weird way.

The neck and back were smooth and white; it looked plastic, but when Rey touched it, it was a harder material. It gave her the creeps and she pulled back her hand.

The face was that of a male, the coloring was slightly darker and more of a shade of gray. The mouth was closed, as were the eyes. And just like a mannequin it was expressionless with vague human features.

"What do you think it is?" Rey asked.

"Nothing," Nate replied. He tapped on it. "It's heavy but sounds hollow."

"What is it doing here?"

"I think someone just had a weird sense of humor. It reminds me of those new mannequins they used that weren't male or female, nondescript, you know."

"Yeah. Scared the hell out of me when I saw it."

"I bet." Nate exhaled. "Well, there's nothing here. Did you find anything else in the back?"

"No. It's empty. The blood tubes I found were the same as the bread date."

"So no answers here. We'll move on."

"What about him?" Rey pointed to the head.

"Leave it. I don't think the others would find it very funny. Let's check the vet clinic. Maybe something is there."

Rey doubted it, but it was worth a shot. She looked forward to checking out the market which was on the next block.

Chalking the urgent care up to a loss, she and Nate left the clinic to try elsewhere.

Another exercise bracelet? Tucker saw the edge of it sticking out of the ground. He didn't understand why he spotted it so easily. But there it was.

Using his fingers, he dug around it and lifted the object into his grip. "Hey, guys, I found another one." He dusted it off and put it in the small bag he carried strapped across his chest.

"Why are you making such a big deal about those?" Sam asked.

"Because it's the fourth one. Second today. Don't you guys find it odd?"

Finch shook his head. "Not at all. People were wearing them for decades when we left. They just aren't biodegradable. That's why you're finding them."

"Maybe. And maybe Fort Collins was a big fitness place. Who knew?" Tucker shrugged.

They were combing through the block before the school—a mix of houses and small businesses—trying to find information about what had occurred.

After the bodies at the stadium and the charred pits, they found nothing else. No answers that were any different. Nothing new.

It was clear that a lot of the businesses had either closed down, or whatever happened occurred at night when they were closed.

It was obvious, at least to Tucker, that sooner or later they would have to admit defeat and hope that he was right about that farm.

The answers could lie with the people there, if they were still alive.

Tucker was sure they were; from the imaging the farm looked too well maintained.

Then again, the images were deceiving. He'd seen nothing on them that looked like a giant body bag or burned body pit circles.

"Let's finish this up," Finch said. "Wrap if for the day, call Rey and Nate back to camp."

Tucker nodded his agreement.

There were three stores right before them. A video game store, beauty salon, and convenience store.

"Why don't we each take one," Tucker suggested. "I'll take the convenience store."

The decision to check the convenience store wasn't random to Tucker. He saw something about it that seemed off.

Finch and Sam seemed to have the attitude that Tucker was looking into things too much or making a fuss out of nothing, but that store...there was something about it.

The gas pumps were nearly gone. Only a bit of one remained. In the small lot of the convenience store, mixed in with all the foliage were products. Canned goods and bottles were scattered about.

The front window was broken, like every other one. The building was overgrown with vines, but there was a huge black mark on the brick above where the big front window was.

As soon as Tucker stepped in the store, he knew something had occurred there.

The shelves had been knocked over, the merchandise that hadn't broken down from time was everywhere, and things looked burnt. Not completely, almost like a flash fire that extinguished as fast as it started.

He scuffled items away with his foot as he made his way to the back and that was when he saw the back wall.

There was a huge hole that was black around the edges.

Clearly something had exploded. It took a second for Tucker to realize the wall didn't seem right.

When he looked inside, he realized it had been put up over the cooler doors.

Another fake wall?

Why?

Tucker stepped through.

What was up with his friend?

Sam couldn't explain Tucker's sudden change of behavior to Finch, nor did he understand it himself.

While he hadn't known Tucker that long, what he did know from being around him and reading about him, was that Tucker was a carefree guy.

He was always upbeat and positive. Yet, the past twenty-four hours had shown a very serious side to Tucker.

He examined everything closely, finding everything he picked up to be of importance and part of the puzzle.

Sam understood the infatuation with the exercise bracelets. Even he didn't get why so many were laying around. But the comb and the small metal pipe Tucker had picked up were insignificant. Tiny items he shoved in that bag he carried.

He watched Tucker go into the convenience store. He knew the look on Tucker's face, he'd seen something or thought he did.

Sam gave it a minute before he went into the beauty salon.

He didn't expect to find any information there. After all, why would he?

Strangely, only half the front window was busted, leaving half the jagged window in the frame. Sam used the door; the glass was broken and he was able to reach inside to unlock the latch.

He stepped inside. It was weather worn and most of the suspended ceiling tiles had fallen down. They lay across the floor and receptionist counter, wires and an old pipe dangling down.

It was one of those budget cut shops. Pictures of people with various hairstyles graced the walls.

The weather hadn't been kind to them, some were faded, some hung sideways and broken.

Sam didn't put much stock into finding anything.

He was about to turn around when he thought about the reception desk. It was completely covered in ceiling tile, and with a swipe of his arm he cleared it.

When the tiles fell to the floor, so did the black appointment book. Finally, a paper trail, he thought. Every other place they went there were very few paper trails.

He lifted the appointment book and placed it on the now cleared desk.

Starting at the back, he flipped through until he found a page with writing. Appointments were logged in by hand, most names were faded, but still readable. The dates stayed consistent with the dates Rey gave.

It was sometime at the end of May that everything had happened.

Looking at the book was the first clue that whatever happened, happened over a short span of time.

The last day with writing had two appointments, the day before six, and for a week before that it was minimal. As he went back farther, he saw the time slots were full, until he arrived in early April.

That was it.

That was when Sam saw his biggest clue yet. Of all the places they were, homes, businesses, it took a little beauty shop to give him some answers.

April fourth.

No appointments.

Just a squiggly line across the time slots and the words "Closed, vaccine day."

Sam's mouth moved slowly as he sputtered the words out loud. "It was a plague." He swiped up the book and raced outside. "Finch! Tucker!"

Finch emerged from the video store. "What is it?"

"Look." Sam showed him the book. "They closed the shop for vaccines. And over six weeks, the appointments trickled down to nothing."

"So it was a sickness they were trying to beat," Finch said.

"It might be." Sam looked up when he saw Tucker approach. His friend looked pale and out of sorts. "Tuck, did you find something?"

"Um, yeah." Tucker patted his bag. "I'm not sure what to make of it. It's a whole situation."

"What is it?" Finch asked.

Tucker pressed his lips together and shook his head. "Not sure. What about you guys?"

Sam held up the book showing him. "Looks like it was a plague or virus."

"Really? Wouldn't there have been like medical stuff set up?" Tucker asked.

"Apparently not," Sam said. "But this doesn't confirm anything, it just lets us know they were fighting something biological. Look, see for yourself what I'm talking about." Sam flipped open the book.

"I'll look at it back at camp," Tucker replied. "Commander, can you radio Rey and Nate. We should head back."

"Sure thing," Finch replied.

Behaving preoccupied and odd, Tucker didn't wait, he just turned and walked away. It was then that Sam saw the bag Tucker carried over his shoulder. It was bulging out a lot more than before he went into that store.

Sam knew Tucker had found something, and with the way he was acting, Sam was willing to bet that whatever Tucker found was more significant than the comb or pipe he had previously picked up.

He'd find out when they got back to camp.

TWENTY-ONE

"As much as I want to say that's what it was," Nate stated, "I can't see it anywhere in this town."

Sam nodded. "But, clearly, whatever it was happened over a short period of time. From April fourth until May twenty-fifth, appointments dwindled. Before that, this shop was always booked."

Nate shook his head. "From what I have seen. It just doesn't add up. In this shop...everywhere."

Finch stood next to Tucker by the inside table, while Rey, Nate, and Sam sat down. "Not disagreeing with you," Finch said, "but explain why you think that."

"Okay so a plague or virus," Nate explained. "Over a hundred thousand people in six weeks dead. From what we have seen, there were no quarantine zones, no cordons. No emergency camps. We didn't get to the hospital, but there was no indication at all at the urgent care that anything happened. No body bags or garbage cans piling up on the roads. If things shut down, so do essential services."

"Someone came in," Finch said, "and cleaned this up. The event happened here."

"So why no quarantine?" Nate said. "They let everyone die? That many people aren't all gonna choose to stay in their homes. They'd overflow the hospitals; emergency hospitals would have to be set up."

Sam said, "We haven't even checked a quarter of this town. We don't know that they aren't out there."

"Plus, it's more than that," Rey added. "I'm not saying people didn't get sick and die, but something big was happening. We hit one grocery store and it wasn't the same. Not at all. The shelves were still stocked but…they weren't organized by product, they were organized by street."

"Boxes," Nate added. "Addresses on them, like one big food bank."

"And the checkout lines were removed. No cash registers," Rey said.

"Okay, I'm playing devil's advocate here," said Finch. "This is after all of us left. How do we know that's just not the way things were in this future?"

"It wasn't that far after us, Finch. Not so much that we got rid of grocery workers," Nate said.

"Why not?" Finch asked. "They got rid of mail carriers after us. If I remember correctly, there were a lot of self-service checkouts in our day. Half, at least."

"What about food issued to homes instead of letting people shop for what they want?" Nate asked.

"We had a food shortage when we left," Finch replied. "It was getting bad."

"Not really," Sam added. "It was resolving nicely thanks to Tucker. When you guys left, they predicted in twenty years the population could starve. Didn't happen thanks to him"—he pointed to Tucker—"and I still think there was a plague or sickness. They tried to be proactive. They had a vaccine day."

Finch nodded. "Could they have been vaccinating for something else?"

"Is there a single scenario you buy?" Nate asked. "You doubt Sam. You doubt us."

"That's not it," Finch said. "I am just being logical. I want the truth just as badly as you do."

"I get it," Rey said. "I do. You're not shooting to be a dick."

"Um…thanks."

"It was just strange," Rey said with a sigh. "The houses got a box each and there was no way to pay. None that we could see. Except four things that looked like bar code scanners. We couldn't tell for sure without power." She looked to the table at the sound of something landing on it.

Five of those exercise bracelets were there.

"Those," Tucker said, "were how people paid. So many of them laying around. That had to be how they did everything. They scanned your bracelet. It's how you paid, showed ID, everything. Bet me."

"Now that," Finch said, "I can buy. Do you have a theory on what happened here?"

"Oh, yeah," Tucker said with certainty. "Everyone in this town, all hundred and some thousand…was killed. Killed, dumped, burned."

Everyone responded with a shocked and disbelieving, "What?"

"On purpose," Tucker said. "In case I didn't imply that enough."

"Okay, wait, what?" Sam blurted out with nearly a laugh. "A plague is hard enough to believe, but you think everyone here was killed on purpose."

"Yep."

"By whom?" Sam asked. "The government?"

"No." Tucker reached into his side bag, pulled out an object and placed it on the table.

"What in God's name?" Nate asked.

It wasn't big—it was part of an arm. Mid forearm, wrist, and hand. But not human. The top of it was dull gray and

153

the underside was shiny and metal. The fingers weren't clunky, in fact they looked intricate.

"Robots," Tucker said.

"You think that belongs to a robot?" Sam asked.

"Yes."

Sam laughed. "That's a prosthetic. You and I both know they had robotic prosthetics."

Tucker shook his head. "I don't think so, Sam. This is really sophisticated."

Nate looked up to Finch. "Anything? Waiting for you to tear this down."

"Oh, I am," Finch said. "Tuck, yeah it looks sophisticated. And even though robotics has been around since at least the 1930 world fair, they had not progressed to the point that they could be killing machines. I mean, for that much of an advancement, humanoid robots would have had to be around when we were on Earth."

"I'm telling you..." Tucker said. "From what I saw they were."

"What did you see?" Sam asked. "Really, what did you see?"

"The bullet holes in the pizza shop," Tucker said. "No bodies or signs of bodies, just the bracelets. Right? We saw that false wall in the garage with a hole in it. Today...in that convenience store was another false wall, with a huge hole blown in it. That's where I found this." He pointed to the arm. "I think it was a trap for the robots. I think some sort of resistance formed and the bracelets were a way for robots to track people and they dropped the bracelets to lure the robots into a trap."

Sam laughed. "This isn't *Terminator*, Tuck."

Finch quickly looked at Rey when he heard her whisper, "Oh my God."

154

"Rey?" Finch called her attention.

"Oh my God," she said with revelation. "I think he's right."

"You too?" Sam asked.

"Yes, me too." She turned to Nate. "You know it."

Nate ran his hand down his face and exhaled dropping his shoulders. "He may be right."

Finch shifted his eyes from Nate to Rey. "What do you two know?"

Whatever happened in Fort Collins had occurred over twenty-five years earlier, but it still didn't stop Finch from wanting to be cautious. It wasn't completely dark, yet he set up perimeters and had Sam and Nate stay behind while Rey led the way to the urgent care.

They went twice.

The first time was for Rey to show them what she and Nate had found, and the second time was for Finch to return to get a dolly.

Tucker spotted a couple of boxes he found interesting.

They took everything back to the Omni where Nate and Sam waited inside.

It was evident that Tucker wanted to drive the point home to his friend and did so with dramatic flare when he set the head on the table with a thump.

Sam jumped back.

"Believe me now?"

TWENTY-TWO

There was a lot of talk when they returned from the urgent care.

Rey knew Sam understood what Tucker was saying about what had been found there. Still, like Finch, he was finding logical explanations because what Tucker was suggesting just wasn't feasible in only seventy-five years. Knowing the state of technology when they left Earth, sure there were robots and possibly they advanced after they left, but to the point where they used artificial intelligence, thought on their own, sought out and killed all people was pushing the limits of believability.

Even for Rey.

But it was still the explanation that made the most sense even if it wasn't probable.

Tucker had found boxes in the storage area by the diagnostics room when he went back.

There were three.

One was open, the other two were sealed, and despite how hard he tried he couldn't find the missing box. He knew there was one because the cartons were marked, 'One of Four,' 'two of four' and so on.

The outside of each box was also labeled, VP-175— Tucker and Sam wanted to know exactly what that was.

Sam was the engineer and dove headfirst into things. Rey figured it was to disprove Tucker's science fiction theory.

After at least two hours of them playing with a tiny square object they found in the open box, trying to figure it out, get it to work, Rey gave up and, like Finch and Nate, went to bed.

It wasn't that it was late, but tomorrow was going to be a long day because in the morning they were heading to that farm.

More so than the boxes, the high school, urgent care, or town, if a farmer lived there then he or she would be the best source of answers, and for that, Rey couldn't wait.

The Omni didn't have much room for sleeping. They were set up for flight, eating, and medical. As far as sleeping, each crew member had their inflatable quarters.

But not everyone felt like setting theirs up.

Not that it was difficult, it wasn't. Finch had erected the outdoor shower stall, which connected to the ship's water supply. Though the water pressure wasn't strong and it was timed for four minutes, it was roomier than the one onboard, less claustrophobic.

Rey took her night shower, hoping it would relax her. It did.

She went on board to find a spot to rest.

Finch was asleep in the pilot's seat with his feet extended to the co-pilot chair and Nate on the bench seating in the dining quarters.

She debated on just stealing Sam's inflatable quarters since his was the only one erected and he seemed preoccupied outside with Tucker. But with the way they were talking back and forth, Rey knew she wouldn't get any rest, so she retreated to the medical bay to crash on the cot.

She found a small bottle that Curt had stashed away in the cabinet under the sink and poured a small night cap. After fifteen minutes of tossing and turning, and trying to block out Sam and Tucker's voices, she finally fell asleep.

It wasn't for long, at least she didn't think so. She was awoken by Tucker's juvenile sounding "ow" along with laughter.

"Too tight?" Sam asked.

"Uh..."

"Let's try it again."

It went quiet, Rey closed her eyes.

"Your pulse is elevated," a strange male voice said.

"Ow," Tucker said.

"Still too tight?" Sam questioned.

"Yeah, just a bit."

"This should do it," Sam said. "Hand out."

"I do not understand why I must keep checking your pulse," the male voice said again. "Is there something you are not telling me?"

"Better," replied Tucker. "I think you have it."

"Have what?" asked the man. "What is better? Are you better, Mr. Milner?"

Rey sat up, swinging her legs over the cot. *What the hell? Mr. Milner?*

"A little, yes," Tucker said.

"I see that this must be an emergency?"

Rey made her way from the medical bay.

"Mr. Milner, would you like me to biopsy that discoloration on your forehead?"

"What? No. That's fine."

Nate was still asleep when Rey passed him. Wires were running across the floor of the ship to the outside, so she followed them.

Sam had two computers set up on a table, but the wires didn't extend to them, they extended to the partially human-looking robot that was sitting on one of the metal storage boxes.

It was dark and the area was lit by dim lights. The mechanical being was white and gray, reminding Rey of a thinner version of the storm troopers, with the exception of the face. It looked even creepier than when she'd found it on the floor. Its eyes moved left to right, blinked, and the plastic face contorted in a mock facial expression.

"Uh, guys?" she called, stepping outside.

"Oh, hey, Rey," Tucker said. "Just in time. We're almost ready to unhook him."

"Yeah," Sam said. "We don't want him to rely on those bracelets. He has to reply to responses."

"Can you do that?" Tucker asked.

"Yep," Sam said. "Just need to program him to ask for information."

"Will he know I'm not Mr. Milner?" Tucker asked as he placed the bracelet back in his bag.

"He will after I reboot him. Which I will. I'm wiping him fresh and we'll start again."

"You guys...you did this?" Rey asked.

Sam nodded. "We did." His finger tapped a key. "It'll be about fifteen minutes. Then Buster is ready to go."

The robot.

"Buster?" Rey asked.

"Yep," Tucker replied. "Thought it fitting since he technically is busted. He's missing the lower portion of his calves and feet. So he can't really move. He tries. His little limbs go back and forth. I don't suppose he was meant to be a big fella. Maybe five feet."

"Okay so…wait," Rey said. "Earlier today you said robots killed everyone, but you built one."

"It was brand new," Tucker said. "Came from a box."

"And," Sam added, "it's a VP. Virtual Physician."

"Why did they call it virtual?" Tucker asked. "That implies it's not real."

"It's not," Sam said. "Check this out, Rey, the manual, which was on that little disk we found, it was called, 'getting to know your Virtual Physician.' He has the equivalent of medical degrees in nine different specialties. Can diagnose, test, treat…"

"And," Tucker added, "the AI was programmed to keep memories, so it thinks it's treated people before. I think these things were supposed to replace doctors."

"But it's still a robot, and you think robots killed everyone."

"Not these ones." Tucker pointed to Buster. "I think there were other ones."

"None of this strikes you as odd?" Rey asked. "You're only fifty years passed when you left and this doesn't seem like way too high tech for you."

"It did at first," said Sam. "Then I saw the components of the bot weren't really that far advanced. I think these were in the works long before we knew about them."

"Like a secret," Tucker replied. "Waiting to be rolled out."

"I don't know," Rey said, walking closer to Buster. "You're keeping him?"

"Absolutely, he can be a great help. I just gotta figure out how to make him mobile."

"I want to look tomorrow," Sam said. "After we go to the farm. I'm thinking I can make him something basic."

"Wish we had his legs though," Tucker said.

"Yeah," Sam agreed. "Like the arms, they probably popped right on."

Rey pointed to the bot. "So this futuristic thing was more than likely already developed when the Omni lifted off. Man, they could have been helpful to the world. We had that doctor shortage."

"Or not," Sam replied. "I think they did finally release the robots, and if Tucker was right, they took over like Terminator or something. This is just a guess."

"That's assuming," Rey said, "they went rogue. If they killed everyone, then we don't know if they were programmed to do it or not."

"This one is not," Sam said. "I saw nothing in the programing that would let me believe otherwise. In fact, ask Tucker, I had data stuff from JAXA and NASA dating back to the early nineteen nineties and this program has a lot of similar basic code."

"So it was around then?" Rey asked.

"No." Sam shook his head. "The materials used to make him are new to me. His power source..." He waved his finger for Rey to follow him and he walked to the back of Buster. "These..." He pointed to three rectangles, six inches wide, one on each shoulder. Then he pointed to a similar, yet smaller one on the back of Buster's head. "These are his cells. Even in low level UV, he will charge. They pull out"— Sam demonstrated how they lifted out some—"for full charging and he'll charge faster when he's in reserve and sleep mode. My point is, these are super similar, on a smaller scale, to how it works on this ship. That technology didn't appear until ten years before Omni left. At the earliest. I'm saying the code is basic. Like some old programmer may have helped design him."

"So he may have been designed and built, but unable to power like this…" Rey said.

Sam nodded. "Not too long before Omni."

A slight whirring mechanical noise precluded Buster opening his eyes.

Rey jumped back.

Buster turned his head left to right. "Hello. I am Doctor VP-175, how are you this evening?" He spoke smooth, slow, and with only a slight hint of a computerized voice.

Sam approached him. "We are fine."

"Is this my assignment?" Buster asked. "Am I to administer medical attention in a field situation?"

"No," Sam replied. "You have been assigned to our spaceship. We are part of the crew. I am Sam, this is Rey…" He pointed. "And Tucker."

"We use first names," Tucker said. "You're Buster."

"Very well," Buster replied. "Buster is a fine name. I seem to be missing my lower limbs, Tucker. How shall I move around on the spaceship?"

"We're working on that. Maybe by tomorrow," Tucker said. "Unfortunately, you were the discounted defective model."

"Please do not call me defective. That is offensive since I am physically disabled."

Rey stifled her laugh. As frightening as Buster was to her, she was intrigued. She could only imagine the reactions of Finch and Nate when they saw. She was certain, like her, they would be amazed.

TWENTY-THREE

Rey hadn't known Finch that long, but she had known him long enough to learn he was a man in control. His voice always remained calm, and never projected anything less than the man in charge.

It had been evident from the get-go, through his strength and demeanor, that Finch was meant to be commander.

That was why it was such a shock to Rey when Finch reacted to Buster.

At first it was strange. Like he'd slept in a king-size bed somewhere; he was awake and looked refreshed when he came from the flight room.

Rey didn't expect him to overreact, but she thought a cup of coffee would soften the blow when he saw Buster standing in the hall.

Rey extended a cup to him.

"You're up early," Finch told her, taking his coffee. "Thank you."

"I haven't been to bed."

"Well, that's not exactly going to help. We have a long day."

"True. I wasn't thinking."

"Did you eat yet?" Finch asked, sipping his coffee.

"No, I was waiting for you. Plus, I'm excited to get started."

"We'll do that. I'm going to grab a shower." He set down his cup. "I won't be long."

"Morning, Commander Finch," said Buster.

"Morning," Finch replied and walked out.

Rey waited for it. The second Finch realized not only was there a short, legless robot standing on the ship, but it talked to him.

But he didn't react, not at that moment. She heard him say good morning to Sam and Nate who were outside. Then she heard the water.

Somewhere in that four minutes it must have hit him, because Finch came flying back into the ship, his shirt in hand, body wet from the shower, and his pants barely fastened.

"What…is that?" He pointed at Buster.

Buster replied, "We have not been properly introduced. I am Doctor Buster VP-175, Chief Medical Officer for this mission."

Finch's eyes widened and one word came from his mouth, with the sound and resonance of a scolding parent. "Tucker!"

"What were you thinking?" Finch nearly blasted Tucker and Sam. "Take it apart."

"Sir," Buster spoke. "To disassemble me would be a great disservice to your crew's well-being."

Finch ignored Buster. "Take it apart."

"No," Tucker replied. "I'm sorry, Commander. I won't do it. We worked for a really long time on it."

"I don't care," Finch said. "I am still commander and I am telling you to take it apart."

Sam stepped forward. "Can I ask why?"

"Why?"

"Yeah, Finch," Nate said calmly. "Why?"

"Because it's unnatural," Finch replied. "And it's…it's freaky looking."

"Freaky looking?" Nate asked, then shook his head. "Honestly, Finch, in all the years I have known you that is the most unintelligent explanation you have ever given. Try again. I'm sure if you give a good reason, they'll be happy to take it apart."

"Well…" Tucker said.

"Happy," Nate reiterated, "to take it apart. What is the reason? Other than freaky looking."

"Sir," Buster said. "If this in reference to my physical disability, I assure you Tucker Freeman will be working on a solution today."

"That," Finch replied. "He understands everything. And…Tucker, for crying out loud, you're running around here claiming robots destroyed all life and you build one?"

"This one is different," Tucker said. "I think it's a different model."

"And you know this how?" Finch asked.

"I know, I think, yeah, I know, it's not a killer."

"Commander Finch," said Buster. "I can assure you I am not programed to do any harm. You may look at my coding for reassurance. I am designed to help not harm."

"I don't care," Finch said.

"You seem to be agitated," Buster commented. "Can I offer you a mood stabilizer."

Rey laughed and when Finch gave her a scolding look, she instantly turned serious.

"How about this," Nate said. "How about we go to that farm today. If someone is alive there, surely they'll know about this…model or robot, we hope. At the very least, they're only around thirty miles out, they'll know what happened here. Why don't we leave it until we know if Tucker's theory is correct. If it is and Buster is harmful, they'll take care of it."

"If it helps," Sam said, "he has nothing in him that is remotely like a gun. Although I think he has a laser."

"Oh, oh, a laser," Finch said with sarcasm. "That's not dangerous."

"It is not," Buster replied. "It will be most useful if surgery is needed."

Finch breathed outward sounding frustrated. "We need to eat, pack up, and head out. What do you suppose we do with that while we're gone? I don't want it having access to anything on this ship."

"Commander Finch, do not worry about me," Buster said. "I can reorganize the medical bay, prepare it for mission, and see if there are items we would need to retrieve from a local medical facility."

"No," Finch told it. "I'm sorry but I am not letting you have access to anything onboard if one of us isn't here." He winced. "Oh my God, I'm talking to it."

Sam, with a slight chuckle, lifted his hand. "I will put Buster in rest and reserve mode. Okay? I want to try to get him to full power. He'll be outside the ship to do so."

"That's fine. I'll accept that as long as you assure me he won't wake up and destroy things."

"He won't," Sam replied.

"Then that will work."

"Commander Finch," Buster said. "If you change your mind about the mood stabilizer, just let me know."

Finch grumbled, swiped his mug of coffee, turned, and walked over to the ship.

Rey gave it a moment and followed.

Finch had pulled up a chair from the firepit area and sat down with his back to the ship.

Rey joined him. "Hey."

"Hey."

"For what it's worth, I don't think you need a mood stabilizer." She sat down.

"That's not funny," Finch said. "Do you think I overreacted?"

"Not at all. You're the leader, you have taken on the responsibility for everyone's well-being. Even though you don't have to, you feel responsible."

"I do. I just…it surprises me you're good with this?"

"Remember I was up all night. I woke up hearing them talking to it. I wasn't at first. I was freaked out. It scared me. But the more I learned about it last night, the less I feared it."

"What the hell was something like that doing in this town and at an urgent care? I wonder if there are more—are they all through the hospital?"

"From what I learned last night," Rey said, "and we are still learning, if there are, they are probably just waiting for patients. That's all this thing does. For now."

"What do you mean for now?"

"You really think Sam is gonna let it only be a doctor?" Rey asked. "And trust me, it only does medical. It insisted on examining me last night. Apparently"—she lifted her bent arm, aiming her elbow at Finch—"I have a small benign cyst right here. Strange. He offered to remove it."

"I don't know, Rey." Finch shook his head. "Something doesn't feel about right it."

"It's going to be hard to feel right about anything if we don't find out exactly what happened to this town."

"Agreed," Finch said. "And hopefully it won't be long before we know those answers."

◇◇◇◇◇

Nate didn't want to be a pessimist, so he didn't say anything. They left Fort Collins and things felt bleak as they drove north to find the town. He hoped that he would have seen signs of a quarantine, something to indicate a plague swept through town, but there was nothing.

He wanted to stop at the medical center, but Finch and the others brought up the point that they'd waited long enough to search out that farm. Answers could be there.

He didn't think so, he really didn't.

As they left Fort Collins they saw no more signs of life in the outlying areas than they had in the town.

Untouched by nature's fury, there was no damage that he could see.

Each mile they drove, the roads grew worse. The black-top cracked with weeds that grew as tall as garden hedges in some areas. Everything on the sides of the road was growing quick and out of control. Too fast for the number of years that had passed.

Branches of trees reached across the road as if trying to touch something on the other side. Grass and ragweed grew wild.

It became thicker and thicker each moment they were on that road.

The farm, in his mind, would be a fluke, something nature had protected for some strange reason.

Until they emerged.

Suddenly they went from apocalypse world into what seemed like normality.

The brush, weeds, overgrown trees, even the wildlife growing from the concrete...stopped.

And like a light at the end of a tunnel, they saw what looked like a farm in the distance. Green rolling hills, a patch of bright in a world so dismal. On the right side of the road, there wasn't any overgrowth or brown dead grass, just a huge field of growing corn stalks.

Finch slowed down the buggy then stopped.

Nate looked at him. "What's wrong?"

Finch looked behind him. "I wonder if all that overgrowth was on purpose."

"Like they're hiding?" Nate asked.

"Exactly."

"From what?"

"Maybe," Tucker suggested. "And this is just coming from a man that grew up on a farm, maybe they already have their hands full with the farm, and they stop taking care of the land wherever the farmland stops."

"That's an even better possibility." Finch began to drive again.

A mile down the highway there was a dirt road that seemed to head in the direction of the farm property. A worn wooden gate crossed the road. It wasn't open and wasn't a means of protection at all.

Tucker jumped from the buggy and opened it so they could pass through. The dirt road wound up a slight hill and it turned into a gravel road at the top.

When they reached the top and stopped, Nate saw the house. And set back a couple hundred yards on the property stood a barn.

Nate wanted to stand up, take it all in. He grabbed onto the bar above his head and that was when he saw him.

A man on a horse.

He moved at a slow pace, until it looked like he saw them, and then began moving with the speed of a thoroughbred on a racetrack. He bulleted his way to the buggy.

The horse had barely stopped when an older man dismounted with the agility of a young person.

He looked about seventy, but it was hard to tell. He wore a button-down shirt, jeans, and hat. His excitement turned to stunned and he froze not far from his horse.

"Well," Tucker said, as he got out of the buggy. "This certainly feels like home to me."

He waited for the others and they walked to the man.

"Sir," Finch said, hands raised. "We mean you no harm."

"Oh, I know that," he said, walking to them. "Pardon my being stunned. Genesis or Omni-4?"

"Omni-4," Finch replied with almost confusion to his tone.

"Omni-4." The man extended his hand. "Welcome back."

TWENTY-FOUR

Tucker felt like he was home. Not home like in his Earth time, but back to a time when life was simpler. When he lived on his grandfather's farm and would sit in the large country-style kitchen at table big enough for ten. A homemade table with bench seating.

Conrad was the farmer's name, and he poured what looked like lemonade from a pitcher into each of their glasses.

"I'm afraid I can't offer you anything you haven't had in a long time." Conrad said. "It's a simple life here."

"Do you live here alone, sir?" Finch asked.

"In the house?" Conrad shook his head. "My son and his two children live here. On the property, heaven's no. We have a hundred and twelve people living on the land. Each has their little patch they take care of and everyone helps with the big stuff. Heck, that's how we eat."

"I need to know," Rey said, "do you know how long it's been since we left?"

"Let me think," Conrad said. "I wasn't born when the Omni left. I came three years later, so...seventy-five years."

Finch looked at Rey. "You guessed it. And Conrad, how long have you lived here?"

"All my life."

"And the others?" Finch asked.

"Twenty…" Conrad paused to think. "Twenty-two years, maybe twenty-three, they all retreated here slowly."

Tucker asked, "Retreated?"

"They had to; it was the only way. People fought hard…"

"In Fort Collins?" Nate questioned.

"My guess everywhere. It was worse here when the Risers attacked."

"Oh my God," Rey gasped. "Zombies?"

"Huh?" Conrad asked. "What are you talking about? There's no such thing as zombies. No, the Risers." He looked at their confused faces. "Follow me."

Conrad led them back down the dirt road to the main highway where they went north another three miles.

The area wasn't as overgrown, some brush, but not much.

They parked the buggy and tied the horse to it and Tucker brought them further off the road to where there was a trench.

"This was the final revolt," Conrad explained. "I'm sure there are a few stragglers left, but not in the area. Then again, this is the first time I've been off the farm in years."

In the trench were hundreds, if not a thousand of mechanical parts that were at time robots. Arms, heads, limbs, and torsos scattered about. The trench had grown over quite a bit but they still could be seen. They weren't like Buster, they were all metal. Some silver, some red.

"I told you guys," Tucker said. "See, Sam, this wasn't some sci-fi theory, this is real." He walked closer to get a better look. When he did, there was an electronic grinding sound. Then some of the parts began to move.

Tucker stepped back. "I thought they were dismantled."

"They are," Conrad said. "They can't put themselves back together, but the only way to really shut them down is to remove their power source, but quite frankly we just wanted them out of commission. Strange the reaction...I know this is going to sound foreign to you, but by chance did one of you pick up a black bracelet, kinda hard plastic with three green lights."

Everyone looked at Tucker.

"Oh, you?" Conrad asked. "That's the reason. They're drawn to them. Programed to find them."

Tucker stepped back farther and they stopped moving. "Who programmed them?"

Conrad shrugged. "No one knows. And it's possible that it was no one at all. That they evolved. They were given a type of AI that continuously learns and adapts. Why don't we go back to the house and I'll explain it all."

Everyone seemed to immediately agree with that and followed Conrad back to the buggy. Except Tucker, he stayed a few more minutes and looked at that pit.

Even though he wanted to know more, he was in awe of it and couldn't pull himself away just yet.

"A few years after the Genesis," Conrad explained when they returned, "they started moving people from the north, south, and east, even west. It was done in lottery style, much like with the ARCs. Only people wanted to move instead, they didn't want to get on the ARCs."

"Why?" asked Finch.

"Uncertainty. They knew they weren't going to some far-off planet, they were going to a future Earth and they just didn't want to chance it."

"They knew?" Finch asked. "When did that become common knowledge?"

Conrad shook his head. "Oh, I don't know. I knew my whole life, since I was a boy. I was happy to stay here and when I found out it was safe, well, bingo, I hit the jackpot. But others wanted a piece and it could have worked. The bots were moving everyone efficiently. Folks out this way were not happy though. If you had an extra room, you had to take in people. Just the way it was."

"You mention bots," Sam said. "You mean Risers?"

"No. Risers are a whole different make. Heck, there were all kinds of bots," Conrad said. "Teacher bots, doctor bots, emergency workers, you name it. The Risers were the enforcers, they pretty much replaced the police and military. They got the name Riser because they rose up and thought for themselves. At one point, early on, they were doing good. Weren't harmful. But what they had in AI, they lacked in durability. They weren't built to withstand the elements, and the storms and everything else started wiping out the Risers and every other type of bot outside this area. Only the builder bots were durable for weather."

Nate asked, "Builder bots?"

"Yes, the ones building the ARCs," Conrad explained. "Conditions worsened with disasters, and the amount of people migrating out here dwindled, so they started moving the bots as well. That is when I think things started to unwind."

Nate shook his head. "I was convinced there was a plague of some sorts."

"Oh, there was, a bad one," Conrad stated. "It went on for years. They developed a vaccine and focused it in the safe zone. But it didn't help that much. In fact, the sickness was the trigger that started it. The Risers started killing

174

anyone with a symptom. Didn't matter what it was. Those bracelets gave your health status and transmitted it to the bots. They took you out. Of course, they started taking everything out. Including the medical bots. Especially them because they were trying to help people. Strange."

"They took the people out," Finch said. "We saw bullet holes but no blood, at least any remaining."

"There wouldn't have been any blood," Conrad replied. "The bullets were from humans fighting. The Risers took you out by sending an electrical charge into the bracelet."

Rey looked at Tucker. "Get rid of those bracelets."

Conrad chuckled. "No, you have to be wearing it to work. Has to be touching the skin. And again, I haven't seen a Riser for a while."

"How did you stay alive? I mean, how did they not kill you here?" Finch asked.

"Easy. We didn't have any bracelets," Conrad replied. "That is how they track and see you. You don't wear one, they don't see you. Not sure how that works. Like I said, people fought their way out. I know this, though, the moment you snap that thing off or unhook it, you better run. They knew you'd removed it. They're on you in a minute."

Finch sat back taking it in. "How long had the bots been around?"

"Hmm." Conrad partially whistled as he exhaled. "My whole life. I know my father had several farm bots when I was a kid. Older models from when he was a kid. I don't know for sure. They evolved so much. I thought you guys had one, but maybe I'm wrong. It was before my time. Not sure if the ARCs did. Then again, they left ahead of schedule."

Nate leaned into the table with folded hands. "The ARCs left early?"

"They did. I guess with the disasters increasing and the plague just starting, they took their chances and waited in space for the wormhole to open. I don't even think they were full. Like I said they had a hard time getting people to leave, and they were forcing them. They left ten years early...I remember seeing it in the sky. Of course, I remember them coming back as well. That wasn't too long ago, though. Five years."

"What?" Sam asked in shock. "The ARCs came back? Then they didn't go through the Androski?"

"At least one of them didn't," Conrad said. "I saw it. It flew overhead. I don't know where it landed, though. Too far for us to look and they never came here." He shrugged. "You know what?" He snapped his finger. "One of my farmers, Mr. Lane, he may know. He took a horse and went to the highest point. He may have a good idea where they went." Conrad stood. "Why don't I go fetch him for you."

"That would be fantastic," Finch told him. "Thank you."

"I hope you folks will stay for a meal," Conrad said. "I know people here will be excited to meet you. They used to tell us every twenty-five years, look up, one of them might come through. And...here you are. Gosh darn, they were right." He scratched his head. "Although I can't tell you who told us that. I'll be right back." He walked to the kitchen door and left.

Finch immediately stood with crossed arms and walked to the kitchen window.

"Guys." Tucker stood. "Do you mind if I catch up to Conrad? I really wanna take a look around at this place. Boy, does it bring back memories."

Finch nodded his go ahead.

Nate looked at the door when Tucker walked out. "What the hell is going on here?" he asked. "I mean anyone else

176

find it strange we have futuristic robots seventy-five years after we left, fifty after Sam and Tucker left."

"It's strange, yes," Sam said. "But you have to think, at one time, computers were dinosaurs, then in the span of fifty years, every household had one, plus tablets and phones. It's possible."

"It is," Finch said. "But that is not the case here. We are in a different world."

"What?" Rey asked. "You mean like an alternate universe."

"No. No." Finch shook his head. "A different one than we knew. It's different because things had changed. You heard Conrad. Come on, Sam, there were no farm bots or medical bots when we left. Yet he was a boy, which meant before you left. And the common knowledge that the wormhole was to another time? Was it common knowledge when you left?"

"No." Sam shook his head. "Unless Quinn spread that knowledge around."

"So no," Finch said. "You have the robots, the wormhole information, you have ARCs lifting off ten years earlier when they didn't even think they'd be done in time for the Androski. But that's right, bots were building them. And what about the safe states? I didn't know it, you didn't know it."

"But…" Rey interjected. "Quinn did say when they went to Virginia they found information that they discovered three states were safe, so that's possible."

Again, Finch shook his head. "No, I'm telling you, what we are seeing is not a natural progression."

"What do you think it is?" Rey asked.

"Someone went through the Androski. Someone went through and ended up far enough in the past where they thought they could change things or save people by getting a jumpstart on technology."

177

"We would know," Sam said. "I mean if someone went through and went back before any of us were born, then none of this would be a surprise."

"Not if," Nate said, "they went through the Androski in Earth-175."

"The same one we went through?" Sam asked.

Nate nodded. "They could have gone through a couple of days before us or after us, we wouldn't know the time change or date they went back to."

"How?" Rey asked. "You heard Quinn. The other party from the Genesis took the ship fifteen years ago."

"For what purpose?" Finch said. "I'll tell you. To go through again. By the time they found out anything the Androski had closed, and they knew they had to wait another twenty-five years to go back. We arrived, they left. Whether it was Quinn lying about his ship, the other part of Genesis, the Lola," Finch said. "Hell, one of the ARCs could have gone through."

"That would explain the jump in technology," Sam said. "It would give them an edge. A big edge if the ARC went back to the past."

"Exactly. But it doesn't matter, who, what or how. Bottom line is," Finch said, "someone changed time."

It was a good day. A long one, but informative and fun. Finch couldn't recall the last time his belly felt so full after a good home-cooked meal.

They met a lot of the farm settlers, enjoyed their company. The food was unbelievable and the stories were equally amazing.

Nate recorded some of them because not everyone on the crew got to hear them. Their tales of survival.

One man in particular, Stavon, told them about how his family was forced to take in a stranger and the stranger was sick.

It wasn't the virus, but the Risers weren't programmed to care or know.

That was when Stavon first realized it was the beginning of the end. Risers stormed to the house, electrocuting the sick house guest.

It wasn't long after that Stavon became an active participant in the revolt. Tattoo slash marks on his arms indicated how many Risers he'd taken out.

Nate counted forty-two.

The farm was nice and peaceful, but Finch and his crew were in solidarity that they would not stay.

After they'd found the ARC, they would try to go back again while the Androski was still open.

Another jump, perhaps to a better time. One where they could stay and be as peaceful as Conrad.

The option to stay was there, and they discussed it, but too much destruction and change was on the way.

Maybe it was the wrong decision to keep chancing it, but the way Finch looked at it, what did they have to lose?

The evening was winding down. Finch finished securing everything on the ship. He sipped on some bourbon while making his rounds with his crew.

Hating to admit it, he did find it amusing the way Tucker was with the medical bot. Finch was relieved to find out from Conrad that the medical bots were not harmful.

179

Outside the ship, Tucker stood with Rey while Buster moved back and forth with his shiny red legs that didn't match the rest of his body.

Tucker had bravely retrieved them from the robot grave at the farm.

"I am healed. I am healed," Buster said. "You are a fine physician of machinery."

"Not me," Tucker replied. "It's all Sam. He's the mechanical genius."

"Ah, Commander Finch," said Buster. "I am very pleased that you are welcoming me aboard as Medical Officer."

"Don't thank me," Finch replied.

"Oh, be nice," said Rey. "Buster's a vat. He absorbs all kinds of knowledge. He'll be fine."

"That's what I'm afraid of," Finch replied.

"Hey, Finch," Tucker said. "Can you let him take your pulse."

"Why?"

"We just adjusted his strength and I want to make sure it's not too much."

"Fine." Finch extended his arm. Buster placed a grip on him. The grip tightened some but not too much.

"Commander Finch, your pulse is sixty-eight, blood pressure, one-ten over seventy, oxy pulse, one hundred percent, and blood alcohol level is at point zero two. Seems you are in good shape this evening."

"Thanks."

"My blood alcohol is a point zero seven," said Rey.

"And that means you're cut off." Finch waved a finger. "I'll leave you two to your new friend." He turned to walk back onto the ship, wanting to double-check with Nate who was working on finding the other ARC. As he entered he heard Sam talking.

180

"You're not going to bed, are you?" Sam asked.

Finch stepped back and looked up. "What are you doing up there?"

"Working on the main cells."

"Nothing is wrong is it?" Finch asked.

"No, just tweaking to make it comparable to Lola. I don't want to rely on a slow charge."

"Excellent. Thank you very much." Finch walked on board. He spotted Nate at the computer table. "How's it going?"

"Good. Very good," Nate replied. "Taking into consideration what Mr. Lane told us about the ship he saw heading northwest, I started looking at our images."

"And?"

He changed the image on the screen and pointed. "I think that's it. That's an ARC. There's lots of trees but if I zoom in"—he expanded and zoomed in on the view—"that looks like a fence. If you look close, this isn't a road. Looks like a path the ARC made when it landed."

"Crash landed?"

"I don't know. But we can set down there and take off from there. What do you think?"

"Hard to tell. It's pretty pixelated."

"I'm ninety percent sure it's the ARC," Nate said. "It's four hundred and fifty miles northwest. Definitely have to take the ship."

"That was the plan. Hopefully that's it. We'll know tomorrow."

"Then what?" Nate asked. "We leave again."

"Absolutely. We make another jump. And hopefully end up"—Finch leaned into the screen—"some place better than all this."

"It's Earth, how much better can it be? I'm all for going back through again. It would be better if we could pick where we end up though."

"Nate, that's half the fun. Spin the Androski wheel," Finch said. "Where we stop, nobody knows."

"And you think that sounds fun?"

"It's been very interesting so far. Hasn't it? Set a course, my friend." He gave a tap to Nate's shoulder. "That's where we go tomorrow."

He left Nate alone to finish what he was doing. Finch wanted to check in with Sam one more time before relaxing for the night.

The next day would be interesting and, Finch was sure, their last day on Earth-75.

TWENTY-FIVE

There was no doubt in Finch's mind that the ARC was damaged on landing. It may not have crashed, but it came in rough. Hard enough that it slammed into the ground with enough force to make a shallow crater.

Finch noticed the crater when he brought the Omni down to land. He avoided it, touching down right after.

The landing was easy and he allowed his ship to coast until they closed in on the ARC. He carefully turned the ship around ready for when they took off again. It was tricky, but it was something Finch was getting good at.

Finch made a lot of deductions.

There wasn't a road there when ARC touched down. Something made them have to land.

From what Finch could tell, the ARC, after making impact, slid nearly two thousand feet, clearing the trees and anything in its path as it pushed a mound of dirt.

That mound was now a hillside covered with grass; the end of the ARC nestled against it and had become part of it.

It was quiet.

Dead quiet and any hopes of finding ARC residents were crushed as soon as they laid eyes on the vessel.

It had been abandoned for a short span of time, not years, by the looks of it. A fence had been erected around the area, though not a large one. All along the radius there were cottages, the prefabricated housing units carried on the ARC. Small four-room, easy to assemble shelters. Three barns and what looked like fencing for animals had been set up too.

The grass was only two feet high. But the biggest telltale sign was the rust and exterior wear on the ARC itself.

Two of the bay doors were open. One near the font and the other toward the back.

"It's massive," Rey said.

"Yeah, it is," Tucker replied. "They were building one right on my grandfather's property. I remember how big it seemed then."

"How do you want to do this?" Nate asked Finch.

"I want to find the commander's log. It has to be in there somewhere. Either his quarters or the deck. Nate, why don't you check out what's on the other side of that hill." Finch pointed. "Sam and Tucker, you look around the housing units and farm area. See what you can come up with."

"Gotcha," Tucker replied. "And if it's alright you with, after we're done, I'd like to take a look inside the ARC. See what one looks like."

"Absolutely," Finch replied. "Keep your radios on. Let's find out what happened to everyone."

The crew divided up, with Finch and Rey headed to the ARC.

Finch had never been in an ARC, but he had seen the virtual tours of the models. He knew what to expect. He aimed for the front bay doors because he was certain that was the main entrance. In every photo and model, entering the ARC was like entering a cruise ship. With high ceilings and a wide-open atrium that was made to look like an outdoor experience.

The passenger rooms circled the area and were stories high.

Such wasn't the case when Finch stepped in.

Gone was the beautiful vision he had in his mind.

The trees were dead, the swings on the playground lay on the ground. Windows to passenger rooms were smashed and broken and many of the doors were open.

The fountain that was at the center of the lobby was green and thick; whatever grew in there had started to spread, which was probably the main source of the damp, moldy smell.

"What happened here?" Rey asked.

"That's what we'll find out." Finch turned left to right. "If I'm not mistaken…" He walked a short distance down a hall. "Here." He lifted his hand and cleared away dirt from a map that hung on the wall.

"How did you know that was there?"

"I can't even tell you how many virtual tours of an ARC I took." His fingers smoothed across the map. "Here. The deck and crew quarters are top level. Stairs down this way."

"Let's hope he kept a logbook."

"Every commander or first officer does."

"Do you?"

"Of course. Curt kept it for a while, now I do it. It could be a few sentences or a page. Doesn't matter." Finch pulled out his flashlight. "Let's head up."

The farther down the hall they walked, the darker it grew. Rey pulled out her flashlight as well and walked closely with Finch.

Tucker figured Finch had him checking out the barns and livestock housing because he knew what he was looking at.

And he did. But it didn't take a farm expert to figure out what he did.

The barn wasn't wooden, it was metal and open and easy to see almost every aspect.

"Anything?" Sam asked as he entered the barn.

"Yes." Tucker turned around. "No animals, no remains, and the supply of feed is gone."

"So there weren't animals?"

"Oh there were. They're gone. Someone took them."

"Pretty much what I got from the housing as well. They took off. Left furnishings, but no food. There's not that many units though. So we're talking maybe forty or so people."

"That's nothing compared to what these ships are supposed to carry." Tucker sighed out heavily.

"What's wrong?"

"I just feel a little guilty leaving Buster on board. He could have been out here learning."

Sam laughed. "Buster is fine. Let's head out, find Nate, and go in the ARC."

"Sounds good."

As soon as they stepped out, they saw Nate walking at a brisk pace toward the ARC.

"Hey," Tucker called out. "Wait up."

Nate paused by the door.

Tucker and Sam trotted his way.

"Did you go to the top of the hill?" Tucker asked.

"I did. I have to get Finch," Nate said. "You won't believe what I found."

The deck was uneventful—the equipment was still intact, windows unbroken, and everything was covered in a thick layer of dust.

A complete contrast to the commander's quarters. They went there when they couldn't locate the logbook.

Immediately upon entering they knew it wasn't good.

There were windows in the quarters, no curtains and the room was bright.

They didn't need flashlights.

Old blood stains were smeared across the walls of the main living quarters. The couch cushions were off, pictures on the walls tilted. An obvious struggle had ensued. Following the bloody trail led them to the body of a woman. She lay face down, her arm extended into the bathroom. A black stain surrounded her entire corpse. Her body was decomposed badly and nearly bones with a thin, leather-looking skin covering. She was clothed, and even though very little remained of her, there was no doubt she had been either shot, close range in the back of the head, or bludgeoned violently.

The back of her skull was shattered.

There were partial footprints that stained the dirt-covered floor and they followed them to a closed door.

Finch looked at Rey before he opened it. She nodded her approval.

He grabbed the handle, moved it downward and pushed the door.

It was as if the room had been sealed. Finch felt a bit of pressure release when he opened it and a foul, rank and dusty smell pelted them.

Rey winced and turned her head.

Stepping inside, they found the commander.

His mummified body sat on the bed, slumped with his back against the wall and a gun still in his hand.

He had taken his own life.

Finch stared at him. "Why did he do this? What happened that made him take his own life?"

"You think he put it in the logbook?"

"I would hope he would have at least put something in there that would give us a clue."

"Like the world's longest suicide note? Someone always leaves one. We should start looking for it."

Finch muttered an unconvincing, "Yeah." He didn't hold much hope that they'd find it.

They began searching the room, checking drawers, the desk, closet. It was just when he was about to quit looking in the bedroom that Finch through about what Rey said.

Suicide note.

They usually left a suicide note.

He walked back over to the commander's body and there it was. The gray, metal-covered binder was under his left buttock, partially covered by a blanket.

Finch grabbed it and lifted it.

"Is that it?" Rey asked.

"It is." Finch held it in awe.

"I can't believe they still used paper," Rey told him.

"They have to use something other than computers." He opened the cover. Inside the front cover were multitudes of tiny memory storage disks taped in an orderly fashion. "Jesus."

"What are they?"

"I don't know. And he still wrote in it."

"Okay, you have to go to his last entry. I can't handle the suspense."

"That's a good idea." His fingers moved to the back of the book and he stopped when his radio sounded off.

"Finch," Nate called out. "Hey, where are you guys? We're in some sort of lobby. There's something you need to see."

Finch lifted the radio. "Stay there. We'll be right back down."

"What do you think they found?" Rey asked.

"Only one way to find out." Finch tucked the book under his arm, and with the flashlight on again, he and Rey went to find the others.

It was a solemn moment for the crew of Omni-4. They stood on top of the hill looking down below. It was an area the size of three football fields, and spaced in rows evenly across were graves.

Thousands and thousands of graves.

The grass had grown tall, but the wooden cross markers stood out.

"We know…where a lot of the ARC people went," Nate said. "Not all though. They buried their dead. Now was it when they arrived, or after, or over the five years?"

"This is tragic," Finch said. "The entire reason for the ARCs was to save lives."

"People did live," Tucker replied. "They just didn't think this was the place to be. Maybe it was dangerous or they found a better place and made a pilgrimage there. We know people left."

"You have the answers." Rey pointed to the book Finch still held.

"I think there are a lot of answers other than this book, too," Finch said. "I also think it'll take a lot more time to search than just a few hours. Anyone up for staying one more day?"

"I'm game," Sam said. "There are things we can salvage from here too. I want to check out the medical bay. ARCs kept medical items in storage tanks to preserve shelf life."

"I'd like to also get the hard drives from the navigation and scanning system," Nate said. "They'll have temporary files on them that will give us a clue what they scanned for when they were in space."

"Then we stay." Finch looked out to the graves. "It's the least we can do for these people. Find out why they lost their lives. But I want to set up camp by the ship. Just in case, because you never know if we'll need to get out."

The crew agreed.

There was so much to see on the ARC, so much to learn, but ironically without knowing how much longer the Androski would be open, they didn't have all the time in the world to do it.

TWENTY-SIX

"Okay, just to be clear." Tucker faced Nate and set a plastic box on a counter—a box they'd use to carry items they found on the ARC. "This is the last thing for today."

"Yes," Nate said.

"'Cause if you want to piss around with that navigation drive, you need to get it installed as soon as we get back."

"I know. I know." Nate pointed to a line of monitors. "This is it."

"You sure?"

"Yep."

"Not like the time when you and Sam had me remove the vault block that he was certain was meds and ended up being condoms."

"No, I'm sure, this is it," Nate said. "On a side note. Those condoms could expire."

"Don't understand the need for them." Tucker looked under the counter. "Aw, this is trickier. It's under here. I have to remove the panel."

"Want me to do it?"

"No, something tells me you aren't as fast with a screwdriver as I am."

"Probably not."

Tucker crouched down, paused, and stood back up. "Here." He took off his bag, lifting the strap over his head. "Hold this."

"I can't believe you carry a purse."

"It's a gear bag," Tucker said. "And I am carrying everything else." He cocked an eyebrow.

"Then I'll carry your purse."

"Gear bag."

Nate laughed and placed the strap over his shoulder. "Do you think we can remove one of these ARC monitors? They're really nice."

"Think they're touch screen?"

"Without a doubt."

"Then we'll find a way. Let me get this hard drive." Screwdriver in hand, Tucker climbed under the counter. "All dusty and shit under here."

"Nate, Tucker, come in," Finch called.

"Answer that," Tucker said. "My hands are full."

Nate grabbed the radio. "What's up, Finch?"

"It's almost four o'clock, wrap it up, we want to set up camp for the evening."

"Tell him fifteen minutes we'll be down," Tucker said.

Nate spoke into the radio. "Roger that, Finch. We're grabbing the hard drive. Give us fifteen."

"Sounds good. Out," Finch replied.

Nate put the radio in his pocket. "Is it really gonna take fifteen minutes?"

"No. But you want that monitor, don't you?"

"I do. You...keep doing that. I'm just gonna..." Nate moved about. "See what else is here that we can grab."

Tucker groaned, but he continued working.

"Desperation," Finch said. He flipped a page in the logbook. Rey was sitting next to him, sharing the view of the book as they sat at an old picnic table outside the ARC. "Total desperation, ramblings."

"Looks like he lost it a good week before he took his life," Rey said. "At least he kept writing. What does 'Pinhead ate the worm' even mean?" she asked. "Seriously. Makes me want to jump ahead and watch the deterioration. Something triggered it."

"Without a doubt. All these storage drives. I'm curious what they are."

"Hopefully they'll work with our system," Rey said.

"Sam said he grabbed something already to ensure it."

"So many entries. Years. I mean, is there another book?"

"There might be."

"We should read from this together every night. Make it a routine," Rey suggested. "Like a bedtime story. The tales of the lost ARC."

"My, my." Finch chuckled. "Didn't know there was a romantic side of you."

Rey laughed.

"What's funny?" Sam asked, arms full as he walked by.

Finch looked up. "Nothing in the book. Rey, she's making a joke."

"I wasn't joking," Rey said. "I suggested he and I read from this nightly like a book."

"Bedtime stories?" Sam asked. "Sounds like a nice romantic idea."

"What the hell, guys?" Rey asked. "I'm sure parents didn't look at it that way when they shared a book with their child."

"Oh, so now I'm a father figure?" Finch joked.

Rey, with a smile, shook her head.

"I'm headed to the ship now," Sam said. "I think I have everything I need. I'll check tonight and can come back in the morning before we take off."

"You want this dolly?" Rey pointed to the small, portable dolly by her.

"Nah, leave it for Tucker. I think he has a bunch of stuff."

"We're right behind you," Finch told him. "Just waiting on Tucker and Nate."

Sam nodded and walked off.

Rey had been thumbing through the pages. "Hey, Finch. Look at this."

"What?"

"It's dated two years ago," she said and read aloud. "What have they become? When did it all turn? My head is still reeling from—"

"Hey, guys!" Tucker called out. "Sorry. We're ready now."

Finch turned around. Tucker was carrying not only a box but a large monitor as they walked toward them. "What the hell did you get?"

Tucker pointed to Nate. "It's like he shopped at a thrift store or something. But he can't even carry anything."

"Hey," Nate defended. "I got our purse."

Finch looked at Rey. "Well, remember this page." He pointed down to the logbook. "Let's head back."

Rey closed the book and stood up at the same time as Finch.

"Here," Finch said, moving to Tucker. "Let me help you." He grabbed the monitor, easing the load for Tucker.

"Oh I can see now," Tucker said.

"You think you guys got enough stuff?" Finch asked as they walked back to the Omni.

"I think we have enough to piece things together," Nate replied. "We'll know tonight."

They arrived at the ship as Sam emerged.

"You need help?" Sam asked. "Holy crap, guys. Do we want it inside or you leaving it out for the night?"

"In," Nate replied. "I want to make sure I can get the drive working."

"And look, Sam," Tucker said, "a monitor. Touch screen."

"Ha, ha, ha." Sam took the box from Tucker.

"How's Buster?" Tucker asked.

"In his glory. He's examining that hard drive you got from their med bay," Sam said.

"Oh shit." Rey snapped her finger just as she started to enter the ship. "The dolly."

"Do we need it right now?" Finch asked.

"Nah, we can grab it tomorrow," Rey replied.

"You know what?" Nate said. "I'll get it. I don't want to take a chance on us forgetting it." He stepped back.

"Oh, look at the geo guy doing something," Tucker joked.

Nate laughed and walked with a brisk pace to the dolly.

It was already unfolded and he opted not to fold it back up. Instead, he pushed it at a leisurely pace.

A few steps into his return to the ship, it happened.

He was just pushing it along, hands on the handle, when a high-pitched whistling sound rang out a split second before something blasted through the left side of his belly. Sparks emerged from him and he flew forward a few feet, landing face-first on the ground.

The instant shock of the moment didn't stop Finch from seeing it.

It stood tall in the doorway of the ARC. Red, metallic, and shiny.

It could only be one thing.

A Riser.

"Get in!" Finch ordered Rey. "Sam..." He pulled out his pistol. "Fire up the ship. Now!" He aimed outward at the Riser as it walked toward Nate. He fired at it as he ran.

The shots hit and ricocheted off of the robot. It jerked at each hit it took, but it still kept moving.

Then another appeared and another.

Finch ran, arriving at Nate the same time as Tucker. He kept firing until his clip was empty.

Tucker reached down for Nate.

Weapon still in hand, Finch helped Tucker quickly lift Nate to the dolly. Once he was on, Tucker ran fast and Finch grabbed another clip.

He was moving backwards, shooting as best as he could. But nothing he did made a difference.

Four of them kept coming. They kept firing whatever type of weapon they had but they weren't aiming at Finch. They were aiming at Tucker and Nate.

Halfway down the stairs in front of the door to the ship, Rey waited.

They moved so fast, everything was a blur to Finch.

Before Finch could even lend a hand to his injured friend, Tucker had Nate over his shoulder, and with Rey's help he was on the ship in seconds.

Finch made it up the stairs just as one of the Risers fired. A blast of what seemed like an explosive hit the edge of the door.

He leaped inside, grabbed the rope for the stairs, and pulled them up. "Tucker, the door!"

It was Rey who lunged forward and, using all of her body strength, slid the door closed.

"Latch it!" Finch ordered as he made his way to the front. He heard another shot hit the ship. He didn't know what was happening with Nate, nor did he have time to think about it.

Finch raced to the front of the ship. The system was running, engines firing. He had to get them out and fast.

It was ridiculous for Nate to get the dolly, that was what Rey thought when he'd raced back to retrieve it. After all, at the time they weren't leaving. But she supposed the area with the dolly would be too dark in the evening, and like Nate said, they did stand chance of forgetting it.

When she saw him run back, she'd taken the logbook inside.

Everything was good.

Normal.

In fact, she was thinking about what to make for dinner since it was her turn to cook. Contemplating that, laughing about Buster's robotic enthusiasm for medical stuff, and thinking nothing out of the ordinary when it turned on a dime.

A single gunshot rang out followed by Finch shouting for Sam to fire up the ship.

It was an order Sam didn't instantly follow. Before Rey could register more shots were fired, and Sam raced to the door.

"Oh my God, Nate's been hit."

At that second she expected Sam to run out, but instead he ran to the front of the ship to get it started.

There was a whirling sound as Buster moved behind Rey to the door.

"We cannot hesitate on treatment," Buster said. "It must be done fast."

Rey couldn't even see what happened. By the time she had arrived at the door, they were racing with Nate on the dolly. She climbed down a couple steps to help Tucker.

Finch kept running backwards, firing and finally Rey saw.

They were frightening and still in circulation...the Risers.

It was happening fast.

Tucker carried Nate inside, Finch pulled the stairs, and Rey closed the door.

She could hear the Risers shooting at the ship.

By the time she stepped back from the door, the ship was moving quickly.

"Grab hold of something," Finch ordered over the speaker.

Rey felt the pressure of the ship barreling full speed ahead.

Tucker was on the floor, one hand securing Nate while his leg extended to the wall, bracing himself.

Rey dropped down, pushing her back against the wall and held onto a seat. The ship jolted and bumped as it sped down the uneven path.

Rey closed her eyes when she felt the pressure in her chest as the ship shot upward, faster and at an angle it had never done before. She grasped as tight as she could until she felt them punch through the atmosphere.

When she opened her eyes, Buster had lifted Nate into his robotic arms and moved toward the medical bay with him.

The ship was still slanted, albeit not as much. Rey scurried to her feet, then held on with every step she took on her way to follow Tucker as he rushed to aid Buster with Nate.

When she got to the medical bay, the ship leveled off and it was apparent that Buster didn't need any help.

"Buster, is he...?" Rey asked.

"Do you mean...expired? No. But I must work quickly."

Nate wasn't moving. He lay on his back on a table. Buster's arms moved fast, almost in a blur as he attached an intravenous drip to Nate.

"He's not bleeding," Tucker said. "Why isn't he bleeding?"

"He was struck with an EC7 burst," Buster replied. "He is fortunate it wasn't an EC9, or he wouldn't be with us."

"What is an EC7 burst?" Tucker asked.

"Enforcer control," Buster spoke as he worked. "Designed to produce an injury that will cause death. It was used to extract information from detainees. Their lives were saved if they volunteered the information needed."

"So you can save him?" Tucker asked. "I'm not a medical professional but it looks like that blasted a hole in him."

"They did," Buster said. "I will repair the damage. Rey, I need you on the other table. Hurry. Remove your shirt."

"Excuse me?" Rey asked. "What...me?"

"Of everyone on this ship you are the closest match to him. You share the same blood type and other markers. I need to perform a skin and organ cloning. Please. Hurry."

"Wait," Tucker said. "You can't take her organs, even to help Nate."

"I am not taking her organs; I am cloning them to repair his. We must not wait." He moved backwards, spun around, and retrieved a small rolling table.

"Is that possible?" Tucker asked.

"The procedure has been around for seventy-one years. I assure you it is perfected." He positioned himself between the two tables.

Rey climbed up on the one that was across from Nate and removed her shirt.

As soon as she lay down, Buster's torso opened and from it emerged an eight-inch square object. Out of that ejected two arms thinner than drinking straws. They moved outward like spider legs, each with four prongs on the end.

One arm rested on Nate's wound, the other on Rey's abdomen. She cringed when she felt the pinch.

"This will sting. I am told it is not very painful but now is the time to ask for an anesthetic," Buster said.

"I'm good. Go."

To say she was nervous was an understatement. Her body shivered from cold and nerves, despite how badly she tried to control it.

"My apologies," Buster said. "It is nothing against your bravery, but for the sake of this procedure, I must administer a sedative."

"Go on." Rey nodded. She looked over at Nate.

Poor Nate, he looked pale and was barely breathing. She raised her eyes to Tucker, who stood looking just as nervous. One arm draped across his waist while he bit the nails on his right hand.

Then Finch appeared. "We're steady and on our way...what...what's going on?"

"He's saving Nate's life," Tucker said. "Some sort of cloning transplant thing. Don't ask. Rey's a close match."

"And you just let her do it."

"I'm fine," Rey said.

"No, she is extremely nervous. Her heart rate is too high," Buster said. "Administering sedative now."

Rey felt another pinch.

Finch asked, "Will he make it?"

"I believe so," Buster replied.

"And what about Rey, will she be alright?"

Rey didn't hear the answer to that. The sedative kicked in and she passed right out.

TWENTY-SEVEN

What happened?

Nate remembered getting that dolly and he went from that, to playing with his daughter, to opening his eyes and seeing Tucker.

"Hey, buddy," Tucker said. "How are you feeling?"

"Sore, I think."

"Yeah, you were shot up pretty bad. Took some sort of Riser hit to your belly."

"Why didn't you let me stay dead?" Nate asked.

"You never died."

"Sure I did. I died."

"Nope." Tucker shook his head.

Buster approached. "Your vitals are stable, it may pain you to sit up, but unfortunately, the commander has informed the humans they must place on their life support suits."

"We're going through soon," Tucker said.

"It appears," Buster said, "the transplant was successful. He is not rejecting the organ clones."

"Whose organs were cloned?" Nate asked.

Tucker stepped out of the way.

Rey sat up on the table next to him. She smiled and waved, then cautiously slid down with a wince.

"Can I give you a pain reliever?" Buster asked.

"No, I'll be fine. I'm gonna suit up." She moved slowly. "I'm glad you're okay, Nate."

Nate nodded and gave a closed-mouth smile. Tucker helped him to sit up and then eventually off the table.

"Anything I need to know to help him into his suit?" Tucker asked Buster.

"Just be gentle. I will aid and join you upfront."

"Gonna have to put you in sleep mode, Buster," Tucker told him. "When we go through that wormhole you may fry out if you're on."

"Very well. I can use a nap after all of this excitement." Buster paused. "I have made a joke. Did you not enjoy?"

Tucker just shook his head with a laugh and finished helping Nate.

"There she is," Finch said as Rey entered the flight deck in her suit. "How are you feeling?"

"Like I got punched in the gut, but otherwise fine. Nate is awake," she replied. "He's doing really well. Tucker is helping him suit up."

"It is amazing," Sam said. "That technology is eons beyond what we had."

"Yet," Rey said, "Buster said it's been around for seventy years."

"Crazy," Sam replied. "And there he is...the Androski. Ready for another go through."

"Hopefully, we can stop for a while this time." Rey sat down, placing her helmet on her head. "Did you look at the logbook at all?"

"Not much, just enough to know that a lot of the ARC passengers left because of the Enforcers. They weren't killing them but they were around."

"They wouldn't know to shoot them," Rey said. "They didn't have the bracelets."

"But Nate did," Sam stated. "He had Tucker's bag."

"So that's how they found us," Rey said.

Finch shook his head. "We found them. They came from the ship."

"It's over though," Sam stated. "We're out of there. Onward..." He pointed at the Androski. "To better things." He smiled. "Hopefully."

Sam reached up to the controls above his head. "Six hundred miles to Earth. She looks beautiful."

"That she does," Finch replied and smiled. "Very blue."

The trip through the Androski was seamless. They knew exactly what to do, when to do it, and it was executed like a well-choreographed ballet.

The only thing they didn't expect was to emerge to a view that was much like the one they had originally left.

Finch thought about that when they'd come out on the other side of the wormhole and didn't see the blue planet.

"Where is it?" he'd asked. "Anyone? Do you see?"

"Big blue isn't there," Tucker said.

"Is it maybe where it was at Earth-75?" Finch questioned.

"Negative commander," Tucker said. "It's nowhere visible."

"I have eyes on the sky," said Nate. "Nothing."

At that very second, the first thing that had come to Finch's mind was that they were home.

Back to the beginning. Back to where they had left.

Just like that satellite had made its way to Omni's time, and so did the Omni return.

That was his hope.

"Four hundred miles," Sam said. "We're on the bright side not able to really see any lights or anything."

"Soon enough," Finch replied. "Let's set a course to orbit at one hundred and fifty miles, then after full orbit, drop to forty thousand feet to make a landing."

"Roger that."

Rey leaned forward. "We are landing, right?"

"At this point," Finch said, "we orbit or we land. There's no going back through until we recharge."

"Finch?" Sam said his name with question. "I'm getting static. Sounds like a radio transmission."

"Put it on the overheard."

All that flowed out was crackling and static. It carried on that way for a few minutes then blips of voices cut through. Nothing intelligible.

"See if you can get it better," Finch said.

"I'm trying," Sam replied.

Finch nearly held his breath watching Sam try to tweak the signal. Waiting and hoping for something.

And then...

"—is Houston. We have you. Go ahead."

The entire cabin instantly filled with cheers.

"They know it's us," Finch said confidently. "We're back." He raised his hand to bring silence to the cabin and he lifted the radio. Just as he was about to proudly reply, another voice came over the speaker.

"Yeah, uh Houston, are you seeing anything down there?"

Finch lowered his hand and looked at Sam. "What the hell?"

"Sorry, Endeavor can you repeat what you mean?"

Finch's eyes widened. "The Endeavor? That was a space shuttle."

"Roger that, Houston, do the Russians have anything up here? Over."

"That's a negative, Endeavor."

"Well, you guys are gonna think we're nuts, but...we're seeing a ship of unidentified origins."

"Can you get us a visual, Endeavor?"

"Roger that we'll try."

Tucker called out, "There. I see it. I see the Endeavor."

Sam replied, "They see us."

The Houston command spoke again. "We see it. It is not one of ours."

"We're gonna try to make contact with the craft," the other voice said.

"Roger that. It's a go but keep your distance until we identify it."

"Roger that."

There was silence for a second, then the voice returned. "This is an attempt to reach the unidentified craft. Do you copy?" Pause. "This is Commander Ronald Grabe of the United States Airforce, flying STS-57, on the Endeavor. Do you read?"

Finch hurriedly turned to Rey. "You're a history teacher. When was the Endeavor, STS-57?"

"I...I...don't know." She shook her head. "I'm a teacher. I don't have a database that I can tap into that goes very far back."

"Shit." Tucker rushed to the computer set up by Nate. "We do. Sam and I brought it." His fingers tapped away on the keyboard.

The commander of the Endeavor repeated the call. "We are trying to make contact with the unknown craft, can you identify yourself. We are pulling closer and are not a threat."

Then suddenly Tucker rambled fast and excitedly, "Oh my God. Oh my God. Oh my God."

"What?" Finch asked.

Tucker's eyes widened. "I got it. Space Shuttle Endeavor. Mission STS-57, Commander Ronald Grabe. Finch, that mission launched June twenty-first," he said, "of 1993. We're in 1993."

Finch stared in shock.

"Finch?" Sam called his attention. "What do you want to do? Remain on course. Do we respond? Are we landing?"

"No," Finch answered without hesitation, and hurriedly reached for the control. "We're faster. We lose them. We lose them until...until I can figure out what to do."

"Roger that, Commander, I couldn't agree more." Sam boosted the power on the ship.

Within seconds they not only lost the communication but had lost sight of the Endeavor, moving back out further from Earth.

Finch released the breath he held. His heart beat strongly as he stared at planet Earth. There in space, six hundred miles above the earth's surface, the Omni would stay for a little while. They had to think and act fast. They didn't have the luxury of time or the option of going back through the Androski. Collectively as a crew they would try to figure out how they were going to handle the situation, because eventually, like it or not, they had to land in 1993.

Jacqueline Druga is a native of Pittsburgh, PA. Her works include genres of all types but she favors post-apocalypse and apocalypse writing.

Follow the author:
Facebook: @jacquelinedruga
Twitter: @gojake
Website: www.jacquelinedruga.com

www.vulpine-press.com